His Holiday Pact

Manhattan Holiday Loves, Book 1

By

AYLA ASHER

Contents

Because, sometimes, you just need a sweet, sultry fake relationship holiday romance...

Chapter 1

♥

Kayla sat at the bar between her two best friends, morosely staring into what was left of her beer.

"Want another one?" Joy asked.

"No," Kayla said, chugging the contents. "No matter how much I drink, I'm still dreading the next few months."

"Hey," Laura said, encircling her wrist with her bangled hand and squeezing. "Maybe there's a silver lining here. If Jordan brings home a girl for Thanksgiving and Christmas, maybe your parents will bombard him with questions about marriage and babies. They can totally leave you alone."

"I appreciate your optimism," Kayla said, giving her a sardonic glare, "but there's no way in hell they're going to let me off the hook. They'll certainly grill my brother and Appolonia...or Apple...or whatever her name is, but they'll definitely save some for me. My mother's dream was to have me married off by thirty and I'm three years overdue. A few more and I'm afraid she might become officially unhinged."

"Why is she such a stick in the mud?" Joy asked. "Being single is awesome. I've never felt freer. I can walk around the house naked and I haven't shaved my legs in weeks. It's everything I've ever dreamed of." She gave a wistful smile, white teeth flashing under her blue eyes and long, wispy strawberry-blond hair.

"First of all, *ew*," Laura said, holding up her finger while Joy snickered at her disdain. "And second, our girl here needs to get laid. It's been a while, Kayla. I'm worried it's going to shrivel up and close off completely."

"Okay, enough talk about my vagina. It's doing just fine, thank you. I have several vibrators and they always find my spot and never ask me to pay for dinner. What more can a girl ask for?"

"Wow," Laura said, finishing her vodka soda. "Our bar is incredibly low. Welcome to dating in the modern world."

"Seriously," Kayla muttered.

After paying the tab, they each headed out of the Hell's Kitchen bar. Laura pulled out her phone to call a rideshare, and Joy and Kayla waited until she'd been safely picked up by Joaquin in a black Camry. Laura lived on the Upper East Side, while Kayla and Joy only lived a few blocks from the bar. They strolled, chatting until they reached Joy's apartment.

"See you at Brandon's party next weekend. It should be fun." Joy said, giving her a hug.

"We'll see. He's been kind of weird since we're both up for the same promotion. I hope he chills out." Kayla's eyebrows drew together. "He was the first friend I made at the firm. I don't want to lose him."

"It'll all work out. Besides, no one 'lawyers' like you," Joy said, making quotation marks with her fingers. "You've got this."

Kayla laughed. "I'm not sure that's the right phrasing of the word, but I appreciate the sentiment. Thanks, J."

Joy smiled, waving before she headed up the steps to her building. Kayla thrust her hands in the pockets of her coat, shivering a bit in the early November breeze. The holidays would arrive soon and, along with them, the dreaded trips home to see her family in New Jersey. To say that her mother was on her ass about finding a man and settling down would be an understatement.

Kayla had dated several men over the years, becoming serious with some, but she'd never made the leap to full-blown long-term relationship. Most of the guys were duds, lost in the sea of beautiful, successful women that comprised Manhattan. The ratio of men to women was so unbalanced that most men moved on at the slightest loss of interest or sign of a problem. And why not, when their Tinder profiles were filled with eager, smiling faces, most in their twenties and still a size four?

Kayla had been a size four...when she was twelve. Now, at thirty-three, she hovered between categorizing herself as curvy and slightly overweight. It wasn't like she didn't exercise—hell, she walked all over the damn city and did spin class with Laura twice a week. But her career kept her busy and most of her time was spent working, especially now that she was up for a promotion.

Entering her three-story walk-up building, she took her time, as she always did on the stairs. Otherwise, she would be out of breath when she reached the top, giving *him* the opportunity to make fun of her.

Hoping her insanely annoying—and infuriatingly gorgeous—neighbor wouldn't hear her footsteps, she trudged along. Sure enough, as she crested the top step on the third floor, his doorknob jiggled and the door swung open.

He stepped outside, trash bag in hand, bare-chested. Kayla's mouth watered at his eight-pack and she berated herself for being an idiot. Gray sweatpants sat low on his hips, the V of his abdomen jutting down below the waistband, leading to a sizeable package. Realizing she was staring like a lovelorn twit, she pasted on a fake smile.

"Hello, Carter."

"Hey," he said, lifting the bag. "Garbage duty. You just getting home?"

"Yep," she said, nodding. "Had some drinks with friends."

"Yeah, the hot chick with the bracelets and the blond with the nice smile. I'm still open to a foursome whenever you guys are ready."

Kayla rolled her eyes. "We're all set, thanks." Arching her head toward the door, she asked, "Who's the lucky bimbo tonight? I'm sure she's armed with fake tits and recently whitened teeth. You always manage to find the ones who appear perfect on the outside."

"Jealous, Summers?" he asked, calling her by her last name, which he'd learned three years ago from the label on her mailbox.

She gritted her teeth. "Yes, I love hooking up with men who are incapable of sleeping with me more than once. You have to be running out of excuses to cut your conquests loose after one night. What will you do if one actually wants to date you?"

Carter gave a *pfft*. "Never gonna happen. I'm honest with every woman I approach. I'd say that's more noble than leading someone on. I like to have fun, Kayla. You should try it sometime. It might get rid of that crease above your nose." He pinched the bridge of his nose between his eyes, wiggling his fingers as he teased her.

"Thanks for the commentary on my appearance. I already understand I'm a troll to you. Some of us actually have real bodies and real boobs." Thrusting her chin up, she breezed past him, wanting to escape into the confines of her apartment.

"Hey," he said, grabbing her wrist. "I'm not putting down your appearance. I was just joking. Ease up. You're a solid five. Five and a half when you're wearing those sexy boots that always clink on the stairs."

She gave him a glare, tugging her wrist from his grip.

"Joking!" he said, holding up his hands. "Come on, Kayla. Sheesh."

"Carter?" A tall redhead peeked from his open apartment, her long leg snaking around the door as it seemed to glow in the backlight from his kitchen. "I'm getting cold. Are you going to come and warm me up?"

Kayla thought his tongue might actually spool out of his mouth. Rolling her eyes, she continued to her front door, sticking the key inside.

"Yep, just gotta take this out. Be right back." His warm body bracketed Kayla's from behind as he leaned down to whisper in her ear. "I'm sorry if I hurt your feelings. You're cute, Kayla. I was just joking. See ya." He continued down the hall, whistling as he entered the room that held the garbage chute.

Kayla entered her apartment, throwing her bag on the counter and turning on the lights. Remembering his warm breath in her ear, she allowed herself to imagine for one moment that he was breathing words of desire into the sensitive channel as he used that delectable body to make love to her. And then, she stopped the madness. Carter Manheim would never be attracted to someone like her. He seemed to have an endless loop of supermodels and socialites vying for his attention. Sighing, she began preparing for bed.

Once she was underneath the covers, she pulled up a book on her phone, hoping the romance novel would replace the thoughts in her overactive mind. Thoughts of Carter's chest, with its smattering of tiny black hairs and that delicious V that led into his sweat pants.

Groaning, she set the phone on the bedside table and turned off the lamp, pulling the blankets to her chin. A dull thud rapped against the wall, and she drew the covers over her ears, trying to dampen the sound. Moments later, loud wails sounded from next door. One female and then one unmistakably male. She could always hear Carter having sex when one of his plethora of women was over. Gritting her teeth, she turned to her side and struggled to push the maddening groans from her consciousness.

At least one of them was getting laid. Unfortunately, it was her hot, arrogant, annoying-as-hell neighbor. Lamenting at the general unfairness of life, Kayla eventually fell to sleep.

Chapter 2

♥

Carter checked his phone and set it back on the nightstand. It was three a.m. and he must've fallen asleep after sexy times with Rhonda the Redhead. The woman had taken everything he'd given her like a champ. He'd give her that.

"Hey, sweetness," he said, jostling her as she lay cuddled against him, fast asleep. Carter didn't do cuddling and he definitely didn't do sleepovers, so it was time for Miss Gorgeous Lips and Sexy Body to hit the road. "I need to get some sleep before work. Do you want me to grab a water for you to take with you?

Her green eyes opened, disoriented as she searched the room. "You're sending me home? Come on, Carter. It's three in the morning. I'll leave when you get up for work."

"Sorry, hon," he said, sitting up and running his hand through his mussed brown hair. "No sleepovers. You know the rules."

Rhonda sat up, her full lips pouty. "Are we really going to do this through the holidays? I thought you were finally coming around, Carter. I want to be with you, especially now that it's almost Thanksgiving. I was thinking of asking you to meet my mother over the holidays."

Red lights flashed as Carter's eyes bugged out of his head. "Excuse me, but what? What do you think we're doing here, Rhonda? I told you I'm not looking for a commitment."

Her eyes narrowed. "Yes, most thirty-five-year-old men say that until they meet the right woman. Don't you want to settle down? Get married? Have kids one day?"

Terror rushed through his body, the thought so perilous that he struggled to swallow. "Honestly, probably not. I might want kids one day, but definitely not any time soon."

"How long are you going to wait?" she asked, lifting her arms in a shrug. "Is this a Charlie Chaplin thing? Do you want to have kids when you're seventy?"

Annoyed, he stood, pulling on his boxer briefs. "Look, I don't know how we devolved into this discussion, but I was very clear with you about what we're doing here. I thought we were on the same page."

She rolled her eyes, standing and beginning to put on her clothes. "I'm twenty-six, Carter. I'm not getting any younger." He scowled. He hadn't asked her age but pegged her around thirty. He couldn't understand being anywhere close to wanting a commitment at her age. Approaching him, now fully dressed, she palmed his cheek. "I've been your booty call for over two months, Carter. Don't you feel anything for me?"

His irises darted over her face and a surge of guilt swept through him. Sadly, he felt nothing but a latent fondness for her. Realizing the turn of his thoughts, her face fell. "I see," she said, nostrils flaring.

"I'm sorry, Rhonda," he said, truly remorseful that she'd developed feelings when he so clearly hadn't. "I tried to be honest with you."

"Yes, you were very honest. I can't dispute that."

"Rhonda—" he said, reaching for her arm. "I didn't want to hurt you."

"Well, you did," she said, striding around him. "You can be honest about not wanting a commitment but people develop feelings,

Carter. Maybe one day, even *you'll* have them. Goodbye." She stalked to the door, slamming it behind her.

Carter sighed, rubbing his finger and thumb into his eye sockets. What was with him lately? He was pissing off women left and right. First, he'd hurt Kayla's feelings with his stupid comments earlier this evening and now he'd hurt Rhonda terribly. Reminding himself that this was why he didn't do relationships, he brushed his teeth and tried to get some sleep before morning came.

C arter was at lunch the next day when the phone rang. Noticing his brother's name on the call log, he lifted it to his ear. "Hey, Ryan. What's up?"

"You busy?"

"No," he said, biting into his chicken wrap. "Just taking a break in between chapters." Carter was an actor, who occasionally did audiobook narration on the side. Today he was narrating a steamy romance novel between a blue alpha alien male and his human female mate. It was actually pretty hot if one was into that sort of thing.

"Dottie called me," Ryan said, his tone cautious.

Carter's heart fell to his knees. "What did she say?"

His brother sighed, sad and morose through the phone. "The cancer's back, Carter. Mom didn't tell us because she didn't want us to worry. Dottie said she only has weeks left and has refused to do chemo again." Silence, thick and heavy, bled through the phone. "It will be her last holiday season with us, Carter. We have to make it special."

Carter exhaled a deep breath, which he didn't realize he'd been holding. "Fuck, Ry. Is there anything we can do to help convince her to do chemo again?"

"I think she's done, bro. Remember the last time? The side effects were terrible. I don't blame her for wanting to avoid that at all costs."

Something burned Carter's eyes and he realized it was the sting of moisture. Closing his lids, he asked, "Why didn't she tell us?"

"Dottie said she doesn't want to ruin the holidays. She wants to remember the last one with us with positivity and cheer. I think she's planning on telling us at Thanksgiving."

Carter nodded into the phone. "Is there anything I can do to make the holiday more special for Mom? If you have any suggestions, I'm open."

Ryan breathed a chuckle across the line. "It's funny. Dottie said that Mom told her you've never brought a girl home for the holidays. She said she wished she'd been able to vet the future Mrs. Manheim. Any prospects you can bring to New Jersey with you?"

Scowling, he thought of the disaster with Rhonda last night. "Nope. My current prospect realized I was a full-blown jerk last night and basically told me to go to hell."

"Yikes."

"Yeah," Carter said, sighing. "Why does Mom get stuck on this stuff? She knows I hate commitment because of Dad. He's a shining example that relationships never work out. Mom's the most amazing woman on the planet. If he couldn't find a way to love her, I don't believe that love truly exists."

"Don't tell my wife that," Ryan muttered. "I'm kind of fond of her."

"Except for Patty," Carter said, smiling. "She's amazing. You got the only one I'd consider making a commitment to. Maybe I can seduce her away from you."

"I'm hanging up now," his brother said, his tone annoyed.

Carter laughed. "Joking man. You make marriage look good. Somehow you got over Dad being a son of a bitch. I just don't think I ever will."

"Well, that's a shame. I know it would make Mom happy for you to bring someone home, if only so she could play the doting mother. But, it's your life and if you're intent on being a proclaimed bachelor, that's your decision. I've got to get back to the office. Sorry to be the bearer of bad news."

"Yeah," Carter said, feeling his eyebrows draw together. "This freaking sucks."

"No shit, bro. It's already so hard to process. Okay, call me when you figure out what time you'll get to Jersey on Thanksgiving. Talk soon."

The line clicked and Carter stuck his phone in his pocket. Finishing the wrap, which now tasted like cardboard, he allowed the realization to wash over him that this would be the last holiday he spent with his mom.

Chapter 3

K ayla stared at the darkening sky as the clouds rolled in for another bout of rain. The day had been dreary, and it got dark so early in November that she might as well be a gnome living under a bridge. It was dreadful.

That, compounded by the fact that her mother was droning on in her ear about Thanksgiving, literally made her want to crawl in a hole and resurface when it was spring and she'd lost fifty pounds to hibernation.

"I'm telling you, dear," her mother's voice chimed from her cell. "Audrey said that her daughter did Peloton for a month and lost twenty-five pounds. It's just fantastic. I'm sure you could do it too."

"Thanks, Mom, but I don't really enjoy throwing money at sexist companies who feature skinny women getting skinner. That's great for Grace," she said, referencing Audrey's daughter, "but not for me."

"Oh, everything's a social justice issue with you, Kayla. Why can't you just try it? You could fit into a size eight by Christmas. Wouldn't that be nice? You might even find a nice man to bring home with you. Jordan's bringing his new girlfriend and we'd love to meet anyone you're dating."

Done with the conversation, Kayla spoke brokenly into the phone. "Can't...hear...service...bad...call later..." With a frustrated press of her thumb, she ended the call. The Irish Bar that sat at the corner of her block seemed to be calling her name and she decided that she definitely deserved a beer after the disastrous conversation. Heading inside, she noticed a few other people at the bar, having a drink after work. Choosing one of the open seats, she smiled at the bartender.

"What'll it be?"

"Snakebite, please. Or maybe you call it a Black Velvet?"

"Half cider, half Guinness. Got it, darlin'. Be right back."

A gust of wind blew her wavy brown hair and she glanced toward the door. Scowling, she saw Carter enter and remove his scarf. Great. He must've had the same longing for a drink as she. Straightening her spine, she hoped like hell he'd ignore her. She was in no mood to talk to anyone after speaking to her mother.

"Hey, neighbor," he said, sitting down beside her as if they'd planned to meet. "Needed a beer, huh?"

"Yep," she said, smiling at the bartender and grasping the pint glass. "It's been a shit day."

"Yeah," he said, his expression thoughtful. "Scotch on the rocks. Macallan twelve if you have it."

"Wow," Kayla muttered into her glass. "Your day seems worse than mine. Scotch, huh?"

He shrugged. "I like the burn. You drinking a half and half?"

"Snakebite," she said.

He nodded, throwing some bills on the counter when the bartender returned with his drink. "To shitty days," he said, lifting his glass.

"To shitty days," she said, clinking. After taking a sip, she asked, "So, why was yours so bad? Did the redhead actually ask you for a date? I know that's your worst nightmare."

His brows drew together as he traced his finger over the rim of his glass. Something in the hunch of his shoulders told her he wasn't down with the jibe. "Sorry," she said, running her hand through her hair. "I'm terrible company right now. My mom just spent ten minutes telling me what a loser I am. Don't mind me." She sipped her drink, wondering if she'd ever seen her usually snarky neighbor so morose.

"It's fine," he said, playing with the tiny red straw in the scotch. "You're right. I don't do relationships. But I found out some news today and now I'm searching my brain for a way I can make things right."

Kayla stayed silent, not wanting to stilt the flow of his cryptic conversation.

His brown eyes slid to hers, and she told herself not to drown in them. She might think he was an ass, but she wasn't blind. He was absolutely gorgeous.

"You see, my mom has cancer and her prognosis isn't good. This will be her last holiday with us."

"Oh, Carter," she said, enclosing his wrist with her fingers and squeezing. "I'm so sorry. That's terrible."

"Yeah," he said, giving a humorless laugh before imbibing the scotch. "She wants me to bring home a girl so she can make sure I'm set up for wedded bliss for the rest of my days." He leaned closer. "The problem is, I have no desire to get married." His tone was sardonic and he gave a little shrug. "So, I'm wondering what the hell to do."

"Mothers like to meddle, for sure," Kayla said, tracing the condensation on her glass with the pad of her finger. "My mom is hell-bent on me bringing someone home. My brother has a new girlfriend and he's four years younger than me. She's distraught that I'm going to end up buried under seven cats while they eat my eyeballs as I drown in the shower because I'm single."

"Whoa," he said, flinching. "That's a pretty intense visual."

Kayla laughed. "Yeah. Accurate though."

They drank in silence a bit, each contemplating the conversation. Finally, Carter said, "You know, an obvious solution would be for us to bring each other home to meet our moms."

Kayla almost choked on her drink. "Excuse me?" she asked, wiping up the droplets she'd spilled with the white square napkin.

"Well," he said, lifting his shoulders. "Why not? We could present ourselves as a couple, each satisfying our mothers' intense and annoying desire to see us with a significant other. It would make them happy while allowing us to get some breathing room."

She tamped down the urge to laugh. "Are you serious? My mother would never believe you're dating me."

"Why?" he asked, seeming genuinely perplexed. "Do you have an extra limb I'm unaware of?"

Kayla gawked at him. "You're insanely hot, Carter. You do commercials for all sorts of toothpastes and tires and insurance companies on television. I, as they say, have a face for radio. My mother would suspect something is up in an instant. Her great hope is that I land someone who doesn't have major facial scarring."

Carter laughed, his perfect white teeth flashing, proving her words as his body shook. "Man, you're funny, Summers. I think you should try stand up. You'd kill on stage."

She shot him a look. "Thanks, but I'm not joking. Like you said, I'm a solid five."

"Hey," he said, grabbing her forearm. "That was an asshole thing for me to say. I regretted it the second the words left my mouth. I was attempting to joke with you but, unfortunately, I don't have your comedic timing." He winked, causing her insides to turn to jelly. "I think you're so cute, Kayla. You have to know that. I love seeing you in those adorable bunny slippers when you take out the trash. I'm always telling my brother about the cute chick that lives next door. Who told you that you were anything but attractive and why the hell did you believe them?"

He looked so sincere, his deep mahogany irises searching hers, and she felt her cheeks warm. "Well, thanks, but there's no way it would work. Thanksgiving is next week and we'd have to work out schedules and all that jazz. It's too complicated."

"What's complicated about it?" he asked, his gorgeous lips pursing. "What time does your family do Thanksgiving dinner?"

"Usually around noon."

"Great. We usually do five p.m. That gives us time to get to both. What about Christmas?"

Kayla bit her lip. "Well, we do Christmas Eve where we open presents and then we usually spend Christmas morning together and have breakfast before I head back to the city."

"You're from Wayne, right?"

She nodded. "Good memory."

"I'm from Pompton Lakes, which isn't too far away. We usually spend Christmas Day together and have a big Christmas dinner, so we could head to my mom's after breakfast with your family."

"Okay, slow down," she said, feeling off-balance by the direction of his thoughts. "I stay over at my parents' house on Christmas Eve. They'd put us in a room together."

"So?" he said, giving a deferent shrug. "I've slept on the floor before. Just don't wear the bunny slippers. I might not be able to stop myself from ravishing you. Like I said, they're hot."

She rolled her eyes, unable to stop the laugh from escaping from her throat. "This is insane, Carter. I can't even believe we're discussing this. Isn't it wrong to deceive them?"

He sighed, clutching his glass. "I don't know. Maybe. I just want to make my mom happy. I know she's bummed that I haven't found love or whatever. She's never understood that I don't want that.

I guess I just figured this would bring her some happiness before she passed on. Maybe I'm just being ridiculous."

Lifting his gaze to hers, he gave a sad smile. "She'd like you. She loves a killer sense of humor."

Kayla studied him, the sad hunch of his shoulders and the forlorn smile on his exquisite lips. Son of a bitch, she wanted to do it. The scheme was all sorts of crazy, but it would actually alleviate a lot of suffering for both of them. In the end, if it brought their parents happiness, was it really such a bad idea?

"Okay," she said before she realized she'd spoken the word. "Let's do it."

"Yeah?" he asked, eyebrows arching. "Are you sure?"

She nodded. "Yep. Let me commit before I chicken out. Once I make a commitment, I never waver. Should we seal it with a shake?" Extending her hand, she waited for him to take it.

He slid his hand over hers, so much larger, the skin warm and smooth. Enveloping her in a firm grasp, he shook, their deal now cemented. Retracting her hand before she did something stupid, like bat her eyelashes at him like a lovesick teenager, she lifted her beer. "To my new fake boyfriend."

Grinning, he clinked his glass with hers. "To my new fake..." he took a sip, seeming to choke on the word, *"girlfriend.* Sorry, new word for me. It's a doozy."

"You've really never had a girlfriend?" she asked, amazed. "You've got to be, like, thirty-seven."

"Ouch," he said, shooting her a look. "I'm thirty-five, thank you very much. And, no, I've never had a girlfriend. Too much drama. You'll be the first one. The first *fake* one, at least."

"Lucky me," she muttered, causing him to chuckle. "So, we should probably come up with a story. How we met, our first date, blah, blah, blah. We need to make it believable."

"Good call. I've got some lines to memorize tonight and this week is busy, but what are you doing on Friday? We could order in and spend some time making up our fake relationship timeline."

"Sounds good to me" she said. "I usually collapse on Fridays because I'm so tired from work. It's usually pizza and PJs."

"Sweet," he said, nodding. "I'll be at your place at seven with pizza in hand. Let me get your number and you can text me what toppings you want." Pulling out his phone, he recorded her number and shot her a text so she had his. "This is going to be fun. I've never hung out with a girl without the possibility of sex. If I'm not careful, this fake relationship is going to seem real."

"You can still have sex when you're in a relationship, Carter," she said, glaring at him. "In fact, if you love someone, I hear the sex is actually better."

His features scrunched. "No, thanks. I like my sex without a side of love."

Kayla couldn't help but laugh. "You're hopeless."

"And you're stuck with me, at least until after Christmas. Hope you can stomach it."

"I'm tough," she said, waving a hand over the bar. "I'll survive."

He chugged the rest of the scotch and rose. "Okay, I've got to get cracking on memorizing those lines. I'll see you on Friday." Leaning down, he spoke in her ear, causing her to shiver from his low tone and warm breath. "And I had no idea you thought I was insanely hot. Try and control yourself around me, okay, Summers?"

She shoved him, shooting him a look of warning as he chuckled. Giving her a wave, he exited the bar.

What the hell had she just agreed to? A fake relationship with her hot-as-hell neighbor? Was she insane? Inhaling a deep breath, she reminded herself that it was for the greater good. It would make both their mothers happy and she certainly wasn't in jeopardy of losing her heart to him. No, the heart that was furiously pumping blood through her entire body as a result of his warm breath in her ear? It would be just fine.

Chugging the contents of her beer, she wondered if she was a genius, a liar or a fool. Only time would tell.

Chapter 4

♥

C arter had a busy week, finishing the audiobook, filming a commercial and auditioning for several more. By the time Friday rolled around, he was beat. Remembering his promise to get pizza, he pulled his phone from his coat when he entered his darkened apartment around five-thirty.

Carter: Okay, Summers. Pepperoni? Mushrooms? Pineapple? (If you say pineapple, I'm calling this whole thing off because that's just gross.)

Kayla: Pepperoni and mushrooms are fine. Should I be offended on behalf of all pineapple pizza lovers, though?

Carter laughed.

Carter: Nope. They've made their bed and must live with their choices. See you around seven.

He changed into sweatpants and a t-shirt, throwing on socks and grabbing a beer from the fridge. Realizing that hanging out with a girl you had no chance of getting lucky with led to wearing extremely comfortable clothing, he lifted his beer toward his reflection in the window. Maybe being in a relationship had *one* advantage. Smiling, he pulled up the delivery app on his phone and ordered the pizza.

It arrived, a few minutes before seven and he headed over to Kayla's. Knocking, he heard her call, "It's open!"

He entered, closing the door behind him and bolting it before setting the box on her island counter. The place was clean, the layout similar to his own, and he smiled at the magnets on her fridge.

"You like the Knicks?" he asked when she walked into the kitchen, staring at the menagerie of magnets that lined the white refrigerator. "Didn't peg you for a basketball fan."

She shooed him away, opening the fridge and pulling out a beer. "Yes, I know it's hard to believe that girls could like anything but painting their nails and waiting to sleep with you, but I do enjoy a good basketball game." She gestured toward the bottles of beer on the shelf. "You want one?"

"I'm good," he said, lifting his own beer. "And I know that girls can like sports, Summers. My mom is a huge Yankees fan. I just didn't know you did. It's cool, although the Knicks suck."

She laughed, nodding as she closed the door and popped the cap from the beer. "They're terrible. But I'm loyal and my dad loves them so here we are." Lifting her hands, she shrugged. "Let me grab some plates. I'm starving."

Setting her beer on the island, she turned and opened one of the cabinets, reaching up to grasp two plates that were stacked high. Carter noticed the sliver of pale skin that peeked out between the thin material of her t-shirt and the waistband of her sweatpants. It was strikingly smooth and an image flashed in his mind of him licking the soft skin. Would it taste like she smelled? Like honeysuckles and jasmine? Strangely, he wanted to find out.

"Earth to Carter," she said, jolting him from the musings. "Here you go. Dig in."

Thrown by the direction of his thoughts, he focused on sliding two pieces of pizza onto his plate. "Your PJs are cute," he said, wondering why his voice sounded so gravelly.

"Oh, I've had these for a hundred years," she said, waving her hand as she perused the pizza, looking for which slices to abscond. "I'd never wear them around a *real* boyfriend, but since you're my fake boyfriend I figured it was fine." She shrugged, giving him a beaming smile, and he noticed how pretty she was with her teeth glowing between her full lips.

Clutching his beer, he gestured toward the couch. "It's okay if we eat on the couch?"

"Yep," she said, following him over after her plate was full and sitting on the plushy cushions. "I always eat here. It's just easier."

They ate in easy silence, her eyes closing in delight when she took the first two bites. "This is good. Where did you get it from?"

"Delenio's a few blocks away. My favorite place."

"Yum. I'll Venmo you for half. Just let me know how much it was."

He nodded, taking another bite, never intending to collect. They might not be dating, but they were having dinner and she was offering her apartment and beer. The least he could do was pay for the pizza.

They eventually finished and cleared the plates. Kayla brought over two fresh beers and sat opposite him on the couch, tucking her bare feet underneath her legs. He noticed she had green polish on her toes and wondered if it was for the holidays.

"You like green?" he said, gesturing with his bottle.

"Oh," she said, extending a leg and wiggling her toes. The action sent all sorts of jolts to his shaft. Feeling uncomfortable, and annoyed that he was, he shifted on the couch as she pondered. "Yeah. I try to mix it up. I'll probably get purple next." She shrugged.

He sipped his drink, wondering why in the hell he was noticing all sorts of sexy things about his neighbor tonight. He'd always thought her extremely cute, but certainly not his type. Maybe it was the comfortability of being in her home, but he felt different tonight, on edge. Chalking it up to the fact that he'd barely had time to jerk off since Rhonda stormed out of his apartment days ago, he inhaled a deep breath, determined to act normal.

"So, let's create the story of how we fell in love," he said. "This should be fun. We can make up anything we want."

"Within reason," she said, arching a dark brow. Her hair was long and wavy and fell thick across her shoulders, touching the tops of her breasts. They were large, and the inner curves barely showed in the window of the V-neck of her t-shirt. Sipping his beer, since his mouth was suddenly dry, he waited for her to speak.

"I think we should say that we got to know each other from being neighbors. Let's keep it as real-life as possible."

He nodded as she continued, chatting as she looked to the ceiling, spinning the story they would tell their parents. They talked for hours, laughing as they concocted tales that were ridiculous but too funny not to joke about.

"So, you're an acrobat who was in Cirque du Soleil and you came home wearing your leotard one night and I had to ravish you?"

Kayla snickered, doubling over on the couch as she clutched her beer. "You can tell your mom it's always been a dream to be with someone who's double-jointed!" They both giggled until the laughter eventually died down and she wiped a tear from her eye.

"Okay, that was fun, but I think we've got it. We met in the building and fell in love at the Irish Pub as we got to know each other. We've been dating for six months and are exclusive. Don't have a heart attack," she said, holding up her palm. "Monogamy will only be mentioned in case of emergency."

Carter felt his eyebrows draw together. "I actually have no problem with monogamy," he said, staring into her deep brown eyes. "I just don't want a commitment."

Her irises darted over his face, studying him. "Okay," she said, drawing out the word. "I'm not quite sure how they're different, but you do you." She sipped her beer, giving him a skeptical look. "We've got the restaurants memorized where we went on our first three dates and all of our subsequent outings including a Yankees and Knicks game. Our dating life is actually hella cool."

Carter breathed a laugh. "It is. We're super fun."

Smiling, she stretched, lifting her arms high in the air, the movement sending all sorts of feelings through his body. "Well, I think we're good. I've got to wash these dishes and head to bed. I've got a long day tomorrow and a party tomorrow night." She stood and padded over to the sink, turning on the faucet and beginning to wash the plates.

"Where's the party?" he asked, making conversation as he approached her. He was done with his beer and should be leaving but, for some reason, he wasn't ready to end their conversation. It had been so easy and Carter found himself wondering when he'd laughed that hard with a woman, if ever. He was usually so concerned with making sure he and his date both got off and then sending her on her way. Somehow, hanging with Kayla felt different.

"Gramercy Park, at my friend Brandon's house."

"Brandon?" Carter asked, arching his eyebrow as he leaned his hip against the sink. "Should I be 'fake' worried?" he asked, making quotation marks with his fingers.

She gave him a morose look. "He's another hottie like you. I'm not even on the radar."

"Uh, is that supposed to make me feel better?"

Kayla laughed, finishing the dish and setting it in the drainer before turning the faucet off. "Well, since you 'fake' seem to care, I have no romantic interest in him. I actually think he'd be a good match for my friend, Laura." At his confused look, she held up her wrist, "Bangle bracelet lady you were dying to have a foursome with last week?"

"Oh, yeah. She's hot." He grinned, loving her instant eye roll.

"I know, believe me. I might as well be a coat rack next to her. Anyway, I invited her. I hope she hits it off with Brandon. We'll see."

Carter studied her, wondering why she continually put herself down. He found her quite attractive, especially her sense of humor, which was wicked. He wanted to ask her but didn't feel the timing was right. Maybe down the road. His gaze drifted to her chest, which was wet from her bout with the dishes. A puckered nipple strained through the gray fabric of her t-shirt and his cock stood to attention. Fuck, was she wearing a bra? Realizing she was, but it was extremely thin, he pushed away from the counter, not wanting her to see the massive erection that was now tenting his sweat pants.

"Thanks for the pizza," she said, striding to the door and unlatching the bolt. Pulling it open, she smiled. This was his cue to leave. Yep, that was right. Nodding, he breezed past her, turning in the hallway outside the door. "I had fun, Summers. You're pretty chill."

She shrugged, giving him another one of those beaming smiles. His heart began to pound in his chest and he struggled with his obvious yet unintended desire for her.

"I'm okay," she said, slowly easing the door shut. "Text me and we'll coordinate getting to New Jersey next week." With that, the door clicked in his face and he was left alone in the sparse hallway.

Gritting his teeth, he headed back to his apartment. After prepping for bed, he shed his clothes, determined to get rid of the raging hard-on that was driving him insane. Grasping his cock with his hand, he began stroking, intending on summoning the image of the hot blond he'd set his sights on when he'd met her in the studio earlier that week.

Instead, an image of Kayla formed, flashing him that gorgeous smile as she grinned up from between his legs. Opening her full, pouty lips, she closed them over his shaft, sliding them up and down, her brown eyes never leaving his. Groaning, he gave in to the fantasy, unable to push her from his mind.

Chapter 5

K ayla popped the bottle of prosecco, expecting Laura and Joy to arrive any minute. Their plan was to get a bit tipsy at Kayla's apartment first, then head to Brandon's party. Joy had already met Brandon twice when Kayla had invited her to after-work drinks in Midtown, but Laura had never met him. As Kayla had indicated to Carter, she hoped they would click and thought they'd make a great couple.

Excited knocks pounded on her door and Kayla opened it to see her two favorite people in the world. The three of them had been friends for years, and Kayla was so thankful she'd met such amazing women in the behemoth that was Manhattan.

"Oh, my god, Kayla," Laura said, eyes wide and cheeks flushed. "Your neighbor is so freaking hot. He was checking the mail and I swear he winked at me."

"Carter?" Kayla asked, already knowing the answer. "He thinks you're hot too. And, ladies, do I have a story to tell you."

The week had been so busy that Kayla had waited to tell her friends about her arrangement with Carter until she could tell them in person. After all, she was pretty sure they were going to be floored.

"Sit, sit," Kayla said, ushering them to the island counter. Once they all sat around the rectangular bar, they lifted their glasses in a toast.

"To making it through the holidays for another year without a man. At this point, we're experts, ladies!" They clinked their glasses and Kayla took a hesitant sip.

"Okay, something's up with K," Joy said, calling her by the first letter of her name as Kayla often did in return. "What gives. You have this shit-eating grin on your face."

"Well," Kayla said, shrugging and running her hand over the smooth counter. "I won't *technically* be single this holiday."

"What in the hell does that *technically* mean?" Laura murmured, her eyebrows drawn together.

"Don't interrupt until I'm finished, okay?" Kayla said. "I don't want a million questions. I'll answer them all at the end."

Her two friends gave each other a look. "She's pregnant," Laura muttered.

"No way. She's boning Brandon," Joy said. "That has to be it."

Kayla rolled her eyes. "I'm not boning anyone." Standing, she lifted her glass. "Ladies, I have entered into a fake relationship with my exceedingly gorgeous neighbor. We're going to pretend to be each other's significant other so our parents will be appeased that we're not washed up old single people."

Laura and Joy's mouths hung open, the champagne glasses frozen in their hands.

"I'm sorry, but what?" Laura asked.

Kayla updated them on the arrangement she'd made with Carter, as well as his mother's illness and their subsequent planning session. When she was finished, she said, "Honestly, I have to say, he's been pretty cool so far. I was beginning to think I hated his guts, but he's actually kind of a nice guy when you spend a little time with him."

"Oh, girl," Joy said, shaking her head. "You're already doomed. Are you listening to yourself? You're already infatuated with him."

Kayla gave a *pfft*, waving her hand. "No way. I have no chance in hell of falling for him since he's a hundred miles out of my league and we have absolutely nothing in common. It's the perfect situation for both of us. I'm actually kind of thrilled he thought of it."

"I bet you are," Laura murmured into her glass. "You'll be even more thrilled when he wraps you up in Grandma's blanket during Christmas at the Summers' and pounds you with what must be his magnificent cock. I mean, he's gotta be six-two and two-hundred-ten at minimum. Do you know how big a cock on someone like that is?"

Kayla rolled her eyes. "I have no interest in seeing his cock," she said, realizing that the statement was perfectly acceptable since it was half true. Okay, forty-five percent true. Still a solid ratio. "We're going to do this to placate our mothers and then we'll move on with our lives. It's brilliant."

"Be careful, Kayla," Joy said, concern in her heart-shaped face and sweet blue eyes. "I don't want you to get hurt."

"I appreciate your concern, but my heart is safe. This is a business decision through and through. Now, enough chatting and more drinking. We have a party to get to."

Worry was evident in their expressions, especially Joy's, but they managed to finish the bottle of prosecco and call a rideshare. Arriving at Brandon's doorman building, they headed inside.

Kayla spotted the host immediately and walked over to introduce her friends. "Hey, Brandon. Thanks so much for having us. You remember Joy and this is Laura."

"Hey, Kayla," he said, giving her a hug. He shook both ladies' hands, his eyes lingering on Laura's extensive silver earrings, which hung to her shoulders beside her flat-ironed long black hair. "Nice earrings."

"Thanks. I got them at Saks. I've never met a sale there I could refuse."

Brandon nodded, taking a sip of his beer. "Well, they're cute," he said, light blue eyes raking over her. "I guess Kayla told you that she and I are up for the same promotion at work. Hopefully, they'll announce it soon so we can get on with our lives. The pressure's been excruciating, especially around the holidays."

Kayla gave him a supportive smile. He seemed to bring up the promotion every time they spoke now, and she missed their easy friendship. Although she wanted the advancement, she certainly didn't want any ill will between them.

"Yeah," she said, wishing to move on from the subject. "I'll be glad when it's over too. Got anything bubbly at this party?"

Brandon nodded, the seriousness of his expression softening a bit. He led them to the kitchen and pointed them to the champagne, telling them to make themselves at home. The party was fun, the three of them making several new friends, and several hours in, Kayla noticed Brandon speaking to Laura as her back rested on the wall, face upturned to his. He was smiling an easy grin and she seemed relaxed and enthralled. Perhaps they'd hit it off after all.

"Okay, I'm definitely drunk," Joy said, leaning her head on Kayla's shoulder as she hiccupped. "I think it's time for Cinderella to leave the ball."

"I'll go with you," Kayla said, chugging the beer she'd been nursing for the past hour. "It's late and I'm beat. Let me tell Laura."

She approached Laura and Brandon, explaining that she and Joy were ready to leave. Laura's brown irises darted between Brandon's and Kayla's until she eventually said, "I think I'm going to stay for another hour. See you on Wednesday for happy hour, right?"

The Wednesday before Thanksgiving was a buzzing night in Manhattan and the three of them always went out for drinks to usher in the holidays. "Sure thing. Have fun. Night, Brandon."

"Night," he said, cordial and smiling. Thrilled Laura was digging him, she gave him a hug. "She's great," she whispered in his ear. "Make sure she gets home safely."

He gave her a squeeze with his arm around her waist, and she and Joy hopped in a rideshare home. Walking up the stairs, Kayla reminded herself to go slowly. Not because she cared if Carter would make an appearance in the hallway—he was most likely banging some chick who was half her size and a foot taller. No, she just didn't want to exert herself. She was a bit tipsy and didn't need to fall down the stairs in her boots.

As she neared the third floor, Carter's door opened and he stood in the doorway, arms crossed over his bare chest, eyebrow arched. He looked like a Greek statue, lean and perfect.

"Can I help you?" she asked, hating that she was slightly panting. From the stairs, of course. Not from his presence.

"You're wearing the sexy boots," he said, grinning. "The ones that make the clinks on the stairs. I'd know that sound anywhere."

Kayla looked down at her black, knee-high boots. They had two-inch heels and were probably the sexiest pair of shoes she'd ever owned. Interested that he'd noticed them, and not just on this occasion, she extended her leg, grabbing the zipper at the top.

"They remind me of Pretty Woman, where Julia Roberts does this sexy zip thing down her whole leg when she's wearing them."

His lips quirked. "Show me."

Understanding that she was now powered by champagne and beer, she giggled and showed a rare confidence. Slowly, she unzipped the boot, sliding the zipper down until the black faux leather flaps hung around her ankles.

"Damn, Summers, that was hot. Do the other one."

Eyes narrowing, she asked, "Don't you have a lady waiting inside who can unzip unlimited pieces of clothing to your heart's content?"

He shook his head, his brown irises simmering into hers. "I took the night off. It's been a long week and I didn't want any distractions. Until you showed up in those sexy-as-hell boots. Do the other one."

The command unlocked something in her and she grinned. Latching onto the other zipper, she slowly lowered it until the black material fell to the ground. Realizing that she was now just standing in unzipped boots, she lowered and slid them off her feet. Gathering them in one hand, she straightened. "Well, was it everything you hoped for?"

"And more," he said, his grin so suggestive she thought it might melt her panties off. "The best part was when you bent over to grab them. I could almost see your nipples. Your breasts are gorgeous, Kayla. Damn." Straightening, he gave her a salute. "Night." Backing inside, the door closed behind him.

Kayla stood dumbstruck, attempting to process what had just happened. Had Carter hit on her? And had she inadvertently put on a strip show for him, even if it was rather benign? Snickering, she realized that was exactly what had happened. And, hell, it had been fun. Entering her apartment, she took her time getting ready for bed, Carter's words lingering in her thoughts. When she lay down to sleep, she slid her hands over her breasts, cupping and squeezing tenderly.

"Carter said my boobs were hot." Giggling, she admitted he was the hottest guy who'd ever complimented her. Reveling in his words, she rolled over and drifted to sleep.

Chapter 6

C arter's work and audition schedule was a bit light Thanksgiving week, understandably, so he tasked himself with cleaning and organizing his apartment. By Wednesday, he was a bit restless and decided he needed to get out of the house. Some of his friends had already left for the holiday, and he hadn't had time to find a new hook up after the disaster with Rhonda, so he was left alone in his apartment with no plans.

Reaching for his phone, he texted Kayla.

Carter: Hey, Summers. What's going on tonight? Want to grab a drink before we put on the show of the century tomorrow?

The text bubble appeared as she typed.

Kayla: I'm actually heading out with my friends. The hot ones. We have Thanksgiving Eve drinks every year.

Disappointment surged through him and he realized he'd been looking forward to hanging with her. Ever since she'd leaned over and given him an eyeful of her gorgeous breasts the other night, his thoughts had drifted to her more than he wanted to admit.

Carter: Is it a chicks-only thing? I can come and be a wingman, but don't want to intrude.

The screen was blank, making him wonder if he appeared desperate. *Hell, Carter, what are you doing? You're now begging chicks* to *hang with them?* Pushing away the thoughts, he read the text that appeared on the screen.

Kayla: I texted the girls and they said it's fine if you come. I think they secretly want to grill you about our little plan anyway. Seven p.m. at Rudy's. I have a few things to finish up but I can meet you at 6:45 in the hallway if you want to walk together. We'll need to swing by and meet Joy on the way.

Carter: Perfect. I'll do my best to be a dutiful wingman. See u at 6:45.

She responded with a thumb's up emoji.

The phone read five-thirty, so he had some time to shower and watch basketball before he needed to meet Kayla. Heading to his bedroom, he sat on the bed, intent on folding the laundry that had been in the basket since Monday. Setting the bin beside him, he began matching up all his socks.

Suddenly, his ears perked as he heard a muffled vibrating sound. Eyes narrowing, his irises darted between the four walls of the room. Where was it coming from? Slowly rising, he walked toward the wall that connected with Kayla's apartment. Aligning his ear with the wall, he listened.

Small, feminine moans reverberated through the wall as the vibrating sound maintained a steady hum. Carter struggled to make out the words, but he was sure he heard an '*Oh, god*" and a "*fuck, yes!*" spattered amongst the groans. Holy shit! Kayla was getting herself off—with the help of a fully powered vibrator. Damn, it was hot as hell. Desire shot straight to his shaft and he emitted a soft groan.

Reaching his hand into his pants, he grabbed his cock, stroking it as he listened through the wall. The pulsations seemed to intensify, causing him to wonder how many settings the contraption had. He'd rarely used sex toys with partners, and certainly was no expert. Kayla's sultry mewls seemed to shoot straight to his dick, and he closed his eyes, gritting his teeth.

Somewhere in the back of his mind, he wondered if he was being a perv, but imagining her lying naked with those gorgeous breasts jutting around her chest as she held the pulsing toy to her clit was too much for him to resist. He was only human and the situation was insanely hot.

As his balls tightened, he realized he was going to shoot his load right into his shorts. Hell, they needed to be washed anyway. Lowering his forehead to the wall, he listened to Kayla moan.

"Oh, god, I'm coming," her sweet voice purred through the wall.

Softly groaning her name, the word a plea on his lips, he began spurting into his shorts. Breathing ragged breaths, he emptied himself as she gave a sultry mewl. Pushing away from the wall, he tossed his shorts and t-shirt in the hamper and entered the shower, unable to control his smile.

Man, that was something. How often did she get herself off like that? Wishing he could join her next time, he told himself to slow down. He'd been thinking a lot about his neighbor ever since their agreement and that wasn't like him. No, Carter usually never focused on one woman, instead wishing to play the field. Why tie yourself to one person when there were so many beautiful women in Manhattan?

But Kayla is different. The sentiment flitted through his mind before he could stop it. As he dressed, he pondered the words, realizing they were true. She was different. She was funny and sexy and obviously smart since she was an attorney. Hell, he'd barely finished his bachelor's degree before moving to Manhattan to make it as an actor. Honestly, Kayla was a catch. Any man would be lucky to have her as his partner.

Shaking his head, he tried to rid it of the madness. The last thing he needed was a partner. No, they were friends who had a common purpose, and after the holidays, they would return to their normal lives where they barely saw each other except for random drive-bys in the hallway.

You can **not** *sleep with your neighbor, Carter.* Repeating the mantra, he dressed in jeans and a light sweater. Sleeping with Kayla would be a disaster. She was the kind of girl you...well, you took home to mom. Not the kind of girl you banged and sent on her way. He liked her and had no desire to make things weird between them. Sex would certainly muddle the easy rapport they'd seemed to build over the past week, and he didn't want to ruin their friendship.

Telling himself he was just horny since he hadn't gotten laid in a few days, he chalked the musings up to his overused and undersexed mind. Hearing a rap on his door, he opened it, finding a smiling Kayla on the other side. Her lips were plump with red lipstick and her cheeks were flushed, probably from her recent shower...or something else.

"Hey," she said, smiling. "Ready to go?"

Carter's heart sank to his knees as he realized the truth. He was in over his head.

Chapter 7

♥

K ayla noticed Carter was being quieter than usual as they strolled down the Manhattan sidewalk. Glancing up at him, she asked, "Is everything okay? You've barely said two words."

"Fine," he said, flashing her one of his gorgeous smiles. "Just thinking about tomorrow. I'm pretty sure Mom's going to break the news to us."

"Sorry," she said, slipping her hand into his and squeezing. "I'll be there if you need me. You can talk to me, Carter."

He squeezed back. "Thanks." They continued walking, neither one releasing their grip. It felt comfortable to Kayla and she told herself not to analyze it. He was going through a huge emotional journey and the least she could do was hold his hand in support.

Eventually, they reached Joy's apartment and she fluttered down the steps. "Hey, guys," she said, her eyes darting to their joined hands.

"Hey," Kayla said, pulling her grip from Carter's and embracing Joy. "Happy almost Thanksgiving."

"Happy holidays, Carter," Joy said. "Haven't seen you in the hallway lately when I come to visit Kayla. You're slacking. We need at least two shirtless runs to the garbage chute per day to meet the quota."

Carter laughed. "I'll strive to do better."

"You do that," she said, giving him a wink.

They continued to the bar, where Laura was waiting outside.

"You two already look like a couple," she said, embracing every-one as she placed an excited kiss on their cheeks. "This fake relationship looks good on you, Kayla."

Embarrassment flooded her cheeks and she tamped down the urge to strangle her friend. "Be careful using the word 'relation-ship' around Carter," Kayla joked. "It causes him to break out in hives."

He lifted his finger in the air. "That is usually true, but with you, it doesn't seem so bad, Summers."

An awkward silence passed between the four of them as Kayla processed his words. "Well, I need a drink," Laura said.

Thank goodness. Her friend had diverted that ridiculously in-tense situation. Strolling inside, they shed their coats and ordered a round.

Two hours later, they were on the way to being happily drunk, Kayla smiling as Joy sang along to the country song on the jukebox.

"Yikes," Carter said, leaning down to speak in Kayla's ear. "Who played country? I'm not a fan."

Kayla almost shivered from his warm breath against her neck. "Joy loves it for some reason. Don't ask me," she said, holding up her hands. "I'm lost as to why."

Carter smiled, lifting his finger and brushing away a strand of hair that had gotten stuck in Kayla's lipstick. The smooth swipe of his skin against hers sent jolts through her body. "Thanks. I rarely wear lipstick. Usually, it's just gloss. My hair's always getting in the way."

"It looks good on you. I like the deep red."

"Thanks," she uttered, taking a sip of her beer. Feeling warm from his proximity, she cleared her throat. "We need to leave at eleven tomorrow morning, right?"

"Yep," he said, nodding. "I'm picking up the Zipcar at nine and then I'll be ready."

"Sweet," she said. "Thanks for making the reservation. I'll just Venmo you half."

He nodded, smiling at her as his eyes darted over her face.

"What?" she asked, squishing her features together. "Do I have something on my face?"

He laughed and shook his head. "You're just pretty cool, Summers. I'm glad we're spending the holidays together."

Her heart slammed in her chest at the reverent words. Although he probably was just trying to be nice, the sentiment drilled deep into her heart. "You're okay too," she said, beaming back at him, trying to retain aloofness. She'd sworn to Laura and Joy that her heart wasn't at risk and she'd do well to remember that. Carter was being nice to her because they had a deal. That was all.

They drank a few more rounds before exhaustion set in. "I've got to go home, guys," Kayla said, yawning. "I'm beat." They all hugged, wishing each other happy Thanksgiving, and her friends informed her they were having one more beer. She shot them an accusatory glare, indicating that she was on to their scheme to have Carter walk her home alone, but they both just stared innocently back at her. Shrugging on her coat, she stepped into the cool air with Carter.

They maintained an easy and flowing conversation on the way home, him asking about her work and her asking about his upcoming commercials. When they reached their building, he walked up the stairs slightly behind her, causing her to wonder if he was staring at her ass. She'd worn a cute skirt and black hose tonight, but her butt was always rounder than she wished and she hoped he didn't think she was gross. Glancing back, he smiled up at her and she let the notion go. Who cared what Carter thought of her ass anyway? They were just friends.

He walked her to her door and she unlocked it, turning to smile up at him. "I had fun. Glad you invited yourself. The girls love you."

Carter chuckled. "I do love putting people in the awkward position of feeling forced to bring me somewhere."

Biting her lip, she felt her heartbeat pick up, blood coursing through her veins.

"Night," she said softly, turning to walk inside. She almost had the door closed when he placed his palm on it, jamming it halfway open.

"Summers?" he asked, a shaft of light from her kitchen wafting over his handsome face.

"Yes?" Her voice sounded gravelly and far away.

"Can you hear me making sounds through the wall that separates our bedrooms?"

She laughed, thinking of all the times she'd heard him having sex with the lady of the moment. "Yep. Sometimes I can. Why?"

Brown irises flitted over her face and he leaned down, causing her to catch her breath. With his lips only an inch from hers, he whispered, "Because I realized today that I can hear you too." Arching his brows, he awaited her reaction.

Kayla's eyes widened as she registered what he was trying to tell her. "No, you can't," she said softly.

His warm chuckle surrounded them. "Oh, yes, I can. It made my day. Hell, I think it made my year. Night." Giving her a wink, he straightened and walked to his apartment, the key jiggling in the lock before he headed inside.

Kayla closed the front door and leaned back against it, letting out a loud curse. Carter had heard her masturbating earlier today. Fuck. Realizing that her life was over since she was certain to die of unresolved embarrassment, she groaned in frustration and headed to bed.

Chapter 8

C arter knocked on her door promptly at eleven a.m. the next morning. Kayla opened it, still wary from his revelation the night before.

"Happy Thanksgiving," he said, thrusting a coffee in her face. "I added milk and sugar. You seemed like the type."

Scowling, she took it and inhaled a sip. It tasted like heaven. "Thanks," she muttered.

His smile was gorgeous with a hint of mischief. "Don't make it weird, Summers. We all get off. We've got a huge undertaking to-day—convincing our families that we're *in love*—" he rolled his eyes and made a funny expression with his perfect features. "C'mon. I've got the Zipcar outside."

Kayla decided to let the embarrassing "worst vibrator session of the year" fail go. She was heading into a long day with a super-hot companion and was excited to see her family. Giving him a grin, she said, "Okay, I'm over it. But just remember that you're a super creeper. I mean, who listens through the wall? Ew."

He breathed a laugh. "Who wouldn't listen?" he murmured, arching a brow.

Shaking her head at his teasing, she grabbed her purse and headed down the stairs with him. Their ride to New Jersey was un-eventful, filled with easy conversation and lots of laughter. About a half an hour in, Kayla realized how much she enjoyed spending time with Carter. He had a great sense of humor and didn't take himself too seriously. It was nice for someone who spent most of her week in a stuffy, buttoned-up law firm. Allowing herself to relax, she settled into their easy flowing conversation.

When they arrived at her home in Wayne, her father immediately appeared on the front step. Once they were parked in the driveway, she rushed toward him, enveloping him in a huge embrace. "Hey, Dad."

"Hey, pumpkin," he said, squeezing her in a bear hug. "You look so pretty."

Her dad had always been her cheerleader, which was welcome due to her mom's lack of approval of her appearance and overall direction of her life thus far. "Thanks. This is Carter."

"Hello, young man," he said, engulfing his hand in a warm shake. "I'm Bob Summers. It's a pleasure to meet you. I'll tell you now that I don't own a shotgun, but if you don't take extra special care of my girl, I'm not above buying one."

Carter held up his hands, palms out. "I have nothing but honorable intentions, Mr. Summers."

"Bob is fine, Carter." Glancing at Kayla, Bob said, "I can see why he's in commercials. Not sure I've ever seen teeth that white. Are they natural?"

"Okay," Kayla said, pushing her dad toward the door. "We're not doing this on the front porch. Let's go inside. Where's Mom?"

"Oh, she's cooking away," Bob said, holding the door so they could step into the foyer. After divesting their coats, they settled into the living room, Carter and Kayla sitting on the plushy couch with white fabric and purple flowers.

"Kayla," her mother said, breezing into the room, large wooden spoon in hand. She was wearing an apron atop beige slacks and a flowing blouse. "I'm right in the middle of prepping, but wanted to say hello." Leaning down, she glanced a kiss on Kayla's cheek. "And you must be Carter."

Carter stood, extending his hand. "Yes, ma'am. Nice to meet you, Mrs. Summers."

"Oh," she said, waving the spoon. "I can't shake right now, but certainly nice to meet you. You can call me Catherine. My goodness, you're such a handsome young man." Her gaze trailed to Kayla. "I didn't realize you'd met someone so attractive, Kayla."

"Well, thank you," Carter said, rubbing the back of his neck. "I like it here. I might need to visit more often. It's great for my ego."

"Yes," Kayla said, standing and rolling her eyes. "My parents are enthralled when overtly attractive people hang with us mere mortals. Let me show you the house."

"Your sarcasm isn't appreciated, Kayla," Catherine said. "And where did you get that blouse? I thought you would've used the gift certificate I gave you from Nordstrom's to buy something nicer to wear for our Thanksgiving meal."

Kayla glanced down at her deep purple, silky blouse. It had a peephole below her throat but was in no way inappropriate. She wore black slacks and cute boots that she'd picked up at a sidewalk sale a few months ago. She'd actually felt good when she'd studied her reflection in the mirror that morning. Of course, five minutes with her mother and any self-confidence was shattered. Shrugging, she said, "I like it. It's from this boutique by my house."

"Well, it makes your shoulders look like a linebacker's. And the pants don't have a crease. Every woman knows that creased pants make one's legs look thinner."

"Okay, Cat," Bob said, standing and sliding his arm around her waist. "It's time for my taste test. It's my favorite part." Waggling his eyebrows, he gently urged her toward the kitchen. She breezed away, bemoaning that she was only trying to help. Approaching Kayla, Bob leaned down and gave her a peck on the forehead.

"I think you look real pretty, pumpkin. Go on and show Carter around. Jordan will be here soon."

Annoyed at her mother, as she usually was, Kayla exhaled a deep breath and smiled at Carter. "Want to see my home?"

Surprising her, he extended his hand. "Sure." She took it, telling herself that it was practical because she could lead him that way. Tugging him toward the foyer, she began the tour of her childhood abode.

Chapter 9

♥

C arter trailed behind Kayla, caught in a wave of sympathy for how her mother had spoken to her. From that brief exchange, he now understood why she was so dismissive of her appearance. How could she not be, being raised by a mother so critical?

As she led him from room to room, then up the stairs to the bedrooms, he listened with half an ear as he studied her. Disagreeing with Catherine's assessment, Carter thought Kayla looked stunning today. Her deep violet blouse brought out the different shades of brown in her shoulder-length, wavy hair and her mahogany eyes seemed to shine above the fabric. The silver bangles at her ears matched the buckle of her belt and the black pants were perfect in his opinion. As he trailed behind her, he realized how snug they were against her gorgeous ass. He'd studied it last night too, as they'd climbed the stairs home, and visions of cupping the generous mounds in his hands had his mouth watering—both last night and currently. Telling himself he would probably go to hell for thinking lascivious thoughts about Kayla in her childhood bedroom, he attempted to squelch them.

After seeing the inside of her home, she led him outside to the expansive back yard. It was well kept and they sat on a wooden swing in the brisk autumn air. Content in her presence, he listened to the songs of the birds as they swayed.

"I didn't get our coats," she said, gazing up at him. "Are you cold?"

"Nah," he said, placing his arm across her shoulders and pulling her close. "I'll just share your body heat. It will help convince the 'rents that we dig each other." She smiled, snuggling into him, and he swore his breath caught in his throat. There, as they rocked under the blue sky and puffy clouds, Carter was overcome with contentment. It wrapped around him like a warm blanket, insulating him from his fears of commitment and intimacy.

Here, holding Kayla against his body, he actually understood why someone would choose to forgo the melee of one-night stands and mindless sex. There was something so comforting about settling in with a person, feeling their smile against your shoulder as you stroked their soft hair.

He hadn't realized that he'd begun trailing his fingers through her thick waves, but she didn't seem to mind as she cuddled into him. Would she be like this after sex? All snuggly and adorable as she tried to burrow into his sated body? Carter had never in his life had the desire to hold someone after sex, but he realized that with Kayla, he wouldn't mind. In fact, he'd love nothing more than to have her magnificent curves and generous breasts smashed against every part of his cooling skin. Nothing would feel more like heaven.

"My mom's a bit of a pill," she said, interrupting his thoughts. "She means well. Dad keeps her in check. He's a ball buster."

"They're both great," Carter said, unable to stop running his fingers through her silky mane. "But your mom must be blind. You look gorgeous today, Summers. I love the shirt. I can see a bit of skin through the peephole. It's scandalous."

Kayla laughed, the vibrations shooting through his body, making him feel so connected to her. "I'm not above causing a bit of a scandal. Especially during the holidays. It keeps everyone on their toes."

Nodding, he leaned his cheek against the crown of her head, wishing her body could stay curled into his for hours. Unfortunately, the sound of a screen door slamming behind them jolted them from their reverie. Turning, he spotted a man walking through the door, a tall, willowy blond woman following behind.

"Hey, sis!" the man said. "Come and meet Appoline."

Kayla stood from the swing, her broad smile magnificent as she waved. "Hey, guys!" As she trailed over to them, Carter felt a cold swell of regret at the loss of her sweet body against his. Straightening his shoulders, he stood to meet Kayla's brother.

Chapter 10

♥

Kayla enjoyed their lunch together immensely. Carter was a fantastic conversationalist, and she'd never experienced so much teasing and laughter at one of their family meals. Unburdened by her mother's endless questions about why she hadn't found a good man yet, thanks to Carter's presence, Kayla was able to relax and appreciate their time together.

She liked Jordan's girlfriend, although she found her to be a bit quiet and shy. Wanting to make her feel comfortable, Kayla made sure to ask her benign questions that would involve her in the conversation. Finally, the meal wound down and they retreated to the living room to have coffee. Eventually, the sun began to crawl toward the horizon, indicating it was time to journey to Carter's house, which was about a twenty-minute ride away. After all the hugs and goodbyes had been dispersed, Kayla hopped in the car with Carter, ready for the next venture in their fake relationship.

"That went better than I could've imagined," she said, gazing over at Carter as he sat behind the wheel. "I should've brought home a fake boyfriend years ago. Wow."

Carter chuckled. "See, Summers? I'm full of brilliant ideas. Just wait, I'm sure there are more in here somewhere." He tapped his head with his knuckles, spurring a laugh from her throat.

When they arrived at his mother's house, Kayla felt the flutter of butterflies in her stomach. Strange, since she had no real connection to Carter or his family, but she realized that she wanted his mother to like her anyway. Hoping she made a good impression, she followed him up the stairs to the red front door.

Pushing inside, he called into the foyer, "Mom? Ryan? You guys here?"

"Carter!" A woman said, bounding up to him and drawing him into a smothering embrace. "You're finally here. Yay!" Pulling back, she extended her hand to Kayla. "You must be Kayla. I'm Patty, Carter's brother's wife. We're all thrilled you're here. You have no idea. Carter's *never* brought a girl home before."

"Patty's one mission in life is to embarrass the hell out of me," Carter joked as Kayla shook her hand. "Great job, woman. So far, you're killing it."

"Oh, stop!" Patty said, playfully swatting his chest. "We're just so happy you found someone who can put up with your difficult ass." Turning to Kayla, she lifted her hand to her face and whispered loudly behind it to Kayla, "You must be a saint. I need details. We'll talk."

"No way," Carter said, drawing Kayla to his side with his arm. "You're not getting anywhere near my girlfriend. I can't have you telling her what a jerk I am. She'll leave me and my heart will never recover."

Kayla's heart slammed at the words, the nearness of his body causing her to shudder. It was the first time he'd actually called her his girlfriend and, although it was bound to happen, it shocked her a bit. Reminding herself that he was an actor, she gave Patty a smile. "Don't worry, I'm a master at gathering intel. We'll definitely talk."

"I like her," Patty said, pointing at Kayla. "This is going to be awesome. Come on," she said, gesturing them down the hallway. "Everyone's in the living room."

Carter hung their coats, and they padded down the hallway to a large sitting room. After meeting Ryan, she turned to a thin woman sitting in one of the leather chairs. "You must be Ms. Manheim. It's so nice to meet you."

"Forgive me if I don't get up, dear," she said, shaking Kayla's hand, her grip thin and weak. "I'm old and my bones creak too much. It's so lovely to meet you."

"You too," Kayla said, sadness swamping her as she realized how frail the woman was. Her sickness was obvious, although she wore a bright smile. Gazing at Carter, she felt a wave of sympathy. Losing a parent to cancer was devastating. Determined to support him through it, she watched as he lovingly hugged his mother and smoothed her brown hair with his fingers.

"You look good, Ma," he said, although there was a latent sadness in his tone.

"I look like an old woman, son," she said, shrugging. "But I'm so happy you're here. And you brought this beautiful young woman home. It's about time. I worry that you're alone in that big city."

"I'm fine, Ma," he said, squeezing her shoulder. Sitting on the couch, Kayla followed and lowered beside him. A woman breezed into the room with short, curly white hair and a brilliant smile. "The turkey is almost ready," she said, plopping in one of the free chairs. "And not a minute too soon. I'm starving."

"This is Dottie," Ryan said, holding Patty's hand as they sat on the loveseat. "She's been my mom's best friend for forty years and lives next door. At this point, she's part of our family. I can't remember a Thanksgiving when you haven't been here, Dottie," he said, looking to the ceiling as he pondered.

"Nope," she said, chuckling. "My first one was years ago, right after you were born, Ryan, and your father was terrified that you weren't going to stop crying so we could sit down and eat. But, eventually, you did and we had a nice meal together. When Carter came a few years later, he was better behaved. I barely remember you crying as a baby."

"Well, obviously, I'm perfect," Carter joked, shrugging as he grinned. "Don't worry, Ry, I'll teach you how. It's not that hard."

Ryan rolled his eyes. "In your dreams, bro."

Laughter filtered through the air as they caught up on life and jobs and the holidays in general. Eventually, Dottie announced that dinner was served, and they filled the seats at the large dining room table.

Wine flowed and food was devoured as they had a fantastic dinner. Kayla remarked that Dottie was an amazing cook and wasn't even ashamed to have seconds. After all, what were the holidays for if not to gain a few pounds? She could join Laura for some extra spin classes in January. It was worth it for the succulent stuffing and pumpkin pie.

After dinner, Carter's mom indicated that she'd like to speak to Ryan and Carter alone, so Kayla and Patty entered the living room, glasses full of wine, while they stayed back in the dining room. Dottie took on the task of cleaning the kitchen, leaving Kayla and Patty to finally have their private conversation.

"So," Patty said, smiling shyly behind her glass. "My husband tells me everything. He and Carter are close. Carter didn't give him all the details, but I understand you all have an agreement to pass as each other's partner during the holidays."

Kayla bit her lip. "Busted. It seemed insane when he first suggested it, and I hate the idea of lying to our families, but I just had the best Thanksgiving meal with my family as an adult. *Ever.* So, as much as I want to feel awful, I don't. Is that terrible?"

"No," Patty said, smiling warmly. "I totally get it. Before I married Ryan my parents had resigned themselves to the fact that I was going to be a spinster with a permanent grandma bun and old-timey spectacles. Thank god I met him and he saved me from disaster." They giggled, acknowledging how ridiculous their parents' notions were.

"I don't mind being single," Kayla said, shrugging. "I have really awesome friends and my life is good. But it's been nice spending time with Carter, even if it's not real."

Patty's eyebrows drew together. "Who says it's not real? I've known Carter a long time and he's not *that* great of an actor." Kayla laughed. "What I saw in the foyer seemed real. He truly seems to like you, Kayla."

"Oh, I think he likes me fine. But I'm not his type as far as the whole dating scene. We've been neighbors for three years. I see the women he brings home. I couldn't hold a candle to them. Hot, sexy actors have a lot of choices in the sea of gorgeous women that comprise Manhattan."

"Hmmm..." she said, staring into her wine. "Well, he's never brought any of *them* home before and Ryan says he pushes everyone away because their dad was an ass and left when they were young. But, he seems comfortable around you. Relaxed. Like his walls are down or something. It's really nice to see."

"Well, like I said, I'm not really a threat to his heart or whatever. One day, he'll bring home one of the perfect tens he seems to gravitate to and then you'll get a real girlfriend. I guess I can say that I'm his practice run. At least I serve a purpose." Grinning, she sipped her wine.

"I don't know you well, so I hope I'm not overstepping, but do you put yourself down like this often? I've known you for two hours and I find you lovely and warm and extremely fun to be around.

Also, I think you're perfectly attractive unless I'm missing some strange growth or something that I'm not seeing."

Kayla laughed. Sitting straighter, she shrugged. "I'm just not, you know, a size four or anything. I think I'm very normal and un-extraordinary, which is totally fine, by the way. My mother wishes I were skinnier and that I took more time on my appearance, but those things just have never mattered a ton to me. I always felt that my brain would get me far in life and the day I passed the bar was, honestly, one of the best days of my life."

"That's awesome," Patty said, lifting her glass in a salute. "I didn't even finish college. Ryan's a Physician's Assistant, so he makes good dough, but my job at the spa does okay. I'm a licensed masseuse and manicurist. I've always felt he was better than me because he's basically a doctor, but he always assures me we're equals. I guess we all have our insecurities."

Kayla studied her light, auburn hair and ocean green eyes, inwardly remarking how attractive and kind she was. "You seem like a great match. You obviously love each other."

Patty's grin lit up the room. "We're obsessed with each other. He's so damn amazing. And hot. He and Carter got their father's looks. I know they're not huge fans of his, but he passed on some damn fine genes."

Kayla couldn't help but agree.

"So, what did your mom say? When you passed the bar. I'm sure she was excited."

Kayla frowned into her glass. "She said, 'That's great, dear. Now you can focus all your time on finding a nice man to marry and start a family with.'"

"Yikes," Patty murmured.

"Yeah," she said, inhaling a deep breath. "And then I think she made some comment about how I should join a nice gym with a personal trainer since I would have the money to afford it."

"Well, I can see where your inner critic comes from. Parents can be maddening, huh?"

"Yeah, but I've gotten to the point where I realize she's the only mom I'm ever going to have and she does mean well. I think she feels like it's her duty to ensure I have someone to take care of me when she passes on." As her gaze trailed to the dining room, she asked, "Do you think she's telling them about the cancer?"

Patty nodded, looking somber. "It's devastating. I wish there was something I could do. But you've made Barbara so happy, coming here with Carter, and I hope you guys can find a way to extend this pretend relationship into something real. I think it's time Carter allows himself to open his heart to someone. He's pretty terrified of it and that makes me sad because he's a fantastic person."

Kayla wanted to tell her that would never happen, and also ask more about why she believed Carter afraid to open himself to someone, but he and Ryan breezed into the room.

"Uh oh," Carter said, looking back and forth between them. "We left these two alone for way too long. How many lurid secrets did she tell you, Kayla? I promise they're all lies."

"Oh, I told her everything," Patty said, rising and patting him on the cheek. "You're in big trouble, mister. She's one blackmail away from owning you."

Carter laughed. "I've got dirt on her too. After all, the walls in our building are paper thin." His irises locked onto Kayla's and she felt herself blushing. "But I won't tell if you don't." He winked, causing her insides to quiver.

Barbara trailed into the room, supported by Dottie, and they settled in for coffee. Around ten o'clock, Kayla couldn't stifle her yawn. Not wanting to be rude, she hid it behind her hand, hoping no one would notice.

"I think Kayla is ready to head home, son," Barbara said, her smile gentle.

"I'm so sorry," she said, shaking her head. "I can stay as long as you want. Don't mind me. I've just had too much wine."

"Then I *really* should take you home," Carter joked beside her. Standing, he extended his hand to her. "Come on, Summers. Let's get you to the carriage that I lovingly call a Zipcar."

After saying their goodbyes, Kayla settled into the car, feeling terrible for ending the evening. "We could've stayed longer. I'm sorry I'm such a grandma. I'm just in a food coma from all the awesome meals today. Man, they were good."

"They were," he said, reaching over to grab her hand. "And don't worry, I was ready too. I'm going to crash so hard tonight." He pulled his hand away to adjust the heat and she missed the feel of his skin against hers. Too tired to focus on conversation, she was glad when he turned up the radio and listened to the Christmas tunes as the car ambled along. She was asleep in minutes.

Suddenly, a warm hand was cupping her face. "Summers? Wake up, hon. We're home."

Lifting her lids, she inhaled a breath and realized they were parked in front of their building. "Oh, crap. I fell asleep. Sorry, Carter. I should've stayed awake and talked to you so you didn't get sleepy too."

"I'm good. No worries. Come on."

They disentangled from the seatbelts and headed up the darkened stairs. Once they were in front of her door, he smiled down at her. "I would say that Step One in Operation: Fake Relationship was a huge success. My mom loved you, Kayla. Thank you."

Compassion pervaded her, along with the desire to know how he was feeling after officially hearing the news from his mother. Wanting to offer him an outlet for his emotions, she asked, "Do you want to come inside for a bit? I'd love to hear how it went with your mom. But only if you want to talk about it."

His eyes darted over her face. "Okay," he said, nodding. "I'd like that."

They entered her kitchen and she gestured to the small wine rack on the counter. "I can open a red."

"Sure," he said, removing his coat and setting at one of the stools at the island.

After opening the bottle, she sat a half-full glass in front of each of them and sat on the stool beside him. "To a successful mission," she said, lifting her glass.

He clinked his against it. "To a successful mission."

Kayla let the silence surround them, sensing he needed a moment to process his feelings. Finally, he said, "They've given her six weeks. So, sometime around the first or second week of January. We talked about the funeral arrangements and her last wishes. It's so fucking hard, Kayla. I don't know how I'm going to do this."

Unable to stop the tears, she let them slide down her cheeks. Grabbing his wrist, she tried to send every ounce of energy from her heart to his. "I'm so sorry, Carter. I don't know what to say. I wish there was something I could do."

His smile was sad as he lifted his hand to her cheek and brushed the wetness with the pad of his thumb. "You did so much today. You have no idea. She was absolutely thrilled that I brought you home. Thank you, Kayla."

Sniffling, she shook her head. "I'll do anything I can. You only have to ask me. I want to support you through this."

He stared at her with such reverence that she thought her heart might pound right out of her chest. It was extremely poignant and she felt so connected to him. "You're such a beautiful person, Kayla," he whispered.

Breathing a laugh, she said, "Well, right now I probably look like a hot mess, but I'm okay."

He shook his head. "You look like an angel." Lowering his thumb to her lip, he stroked it, slow and reverent. "I wondered how soft your lips were." The deep timbre of his voice was mesmerizing. "They're perfect. Fuck," he whispered, the pad of his thumb applying a slight pressure as her mouth opened a bit wider at the urging. "I want to kiss you so badly."

Kayla struggled to breathe, her body throbbing from the blood now furiously pumping through her veins. "We can't," she said, frozen under his touch. "All of this is fake."

"Nothing about you is fake," he said, his gaze cemented to her lips. "I didn't expect this, but it feels so real." Lifting his eyes to hers, he asked, "Do you want me to kiss you, Kayla?"

"No," she whispered, shaking her head slightly.

"Why are you lying?" he asked, the words almost a plea on his lips.

"Because I'm terrified."

A long, slow breath exited his lungs. "So am I. This is confusing as hell."

"I don't want to ruin it, Carter. We still have four weeks 'til Christmas. I don't want to muddy the waters with sex. We need to keep this platonic. Once the holidays are over, we won't need each other anymore."

Lowering his hand to his thigh, he studied her. "I'm not sure that's true."

Her eyebrows drew together. "You think that just because we feel a spark you're going to want to be in a long-term relationship with me? I thought that was the opposite of everything you wanted."

Sighing, he picked up the glass, rotating it before he took a sip. "I don't know what I want anymore. Nothing is clear when the person you love most is dying. I'm a wreck."

"I want to comfort you so badly, but I can't do it with sex, Carter. I'm not that kind of person. I would fall in love with you and you'd break my heart and we'd end up hating each other. I don't want that for us."

Taking another sip, he set the glass on the table and stood. "I hate it when you're smarter than me, which is most of the time, by the way," he said, arching a brow. "Sorry, I didn't mean to make you feel uncomfortable. Forget this ever happened."

Never in a million years, she thought, but felt it best to forge ahead and get them to solid ground again. "It's all good. You didn't make it weird. I'm still here for you and we're still friends. See, that's the power of not having sex."

He chuckled. "Never knew that was a power, but okay. See you soon, Summers. Not sure what you're doing this weekend, but if you want to hang, I'm around. Text me." Grabbing his coat from the edge of the counter, he gave her a salute and left the apartment.

Kayla lifted the glass with shaking hands, sipping the wine as she wondered what the hell had just happened. There was no way in hell Carter was supposed to be attracted to someone like her. He must've been swept away by the emotions surrounding his mother's illness and his need for comfort. Chalking it up to that, she set their glasses in the sink and headed to get ready for bed.

When she pulled her panties off, the wetness that pooled on the fabric was a stark reminder of how ready her body had been to make love to Carter. Tossing them in the hamper, she put on a fresh pair, reminding herself to stay calm and practical. Carter was a master at one-night stands and meaningless sex, but it just wasn't in Kayla's wheelhouse. Getting intimate with someone never came easy to her, with her reservations about her appearance and weight, and making love to him would open her up in ways that would make her extremely vulnerable. She didn't blame him for seeking comfort with her but knew she would always have to be the one who abstained for both of them. A tryst between them would mean nothing to him but, oh, it would mean so much to her. Unable to accept that imbalance, she resolved herself to ensure they remained in the friend zone.

When she lay in bed with darkness surrounding her, she sent a prayer through the wall, hoping it would reach him. Regardless of their strange interaction this evening, she now considered Carter a friend and truly wanted to support him through his mother's illness. Reminding herself to check on him tomorrow, she fell to sleep.

Chapter 11

♥

C arter awoke to a stream of sunlight in his sleep-encrusted eyes and a raging hard-on. Groaning, he pulled the extra pillow to his face, burying his nose in the plush. Realizing he was in one hell of a mood, he growled into the pillow. Throwing it against the wall, he settled into the mattress, annoyed that his first thought was of Kayla.

Kayla, with her wide, wet eyes, so full of caring and compassion. Never had he seen anything more beautiful than her staring into his soul as she'd comforted him last night. And then, he'd gone and almost royally fucked everything up.

His sweet, adorable-as-hell neighbor was not some chick he could just get his rocks off with and move on. He actually *liked* Kayla, and she'd been amazing with his family. If he wasn't a thousand shades of fucked up from his dad's desertion of his mother, he would actually be honored to date her and attempt a normal relationship for the first time in his life. But, he was a mess and had nothing to offer her but sex. Really great, sweaty, open-mouthed, toe-curling, hot sex. Groaning in frustration, he slid his hand to his cock to rid it of the maddening erection.

Once he was up and about, he felt restless so he threw on his sneakers and sweats and headed outside for a jog. The air cleared his head a bit and he told himself to silence the critic in his head.

Kayla had seemed fine and she still wanted to be friends, so he hadn't blown it. He admired her maturity, realizing that she was leagues ahead of him in that area.

Kayla was a loving, amazing woman whom any man would be lucky to have as a partner. He truly hoped that she would find someone someday who would love her with his whole heart. Then, he'd promptly smash the bastard's face in because he couldn't stomach the image of another man making love to her. Feeling his eyebrows draw together, he tried to imagine her head thrown back in ecstasy, those delectable breasts being devoured by someone else's mouth. But, in his vision, his face was the only one he could conjure loving her that way, drawing her nipple between his lips...burying his head between her soft thighs...

Maybe she'd even wear the sexy boots while he licked away every drop of her sweet juices.

Realizing that he was on the path to driving himself insane, he stopped in front of the stoop that led to his building, gasping for air from the run as he intermittently chugged from the water bottle. The main door swung open above and the woman who'd consumed his every thought that morning trailed down the stairs. She looked cute in jeans, furry ankle boots and a sweatshirt that read "Indoorsy".

"Hey," she said, stopping one stair above the ground, putting her at eye level. "How'd you sleep."

"Good," he said, chugging more water since his throat was suddenly dry. Her hair was pulled back into a ponytail, showcasing her prominent cheekbones. She wasn't wearing a stitch of makeup and he noticed how long her lashes were, even without mascara. Most of the women he hooked up with loaded the stuff on or wore fake lashes. It was refreshing to see a woman who was comfortable being natural. "I needed to run off the feast we ate yesterday."

Her brow arched. "I should be doing the same, but I'm heading to the deli to grab coffee and an egg sandwich. It will be killer to my thighs, but it's a holiday weekend and I'm treating myself."

Forcing himself not to gaze at her thighs, although he'd love nothing more than to look at her legs in the tight jeans she wore, he nodded. "Sounds great." Running his hand through his hair, he asked, "Are we cool?"

"Yeah," she said, smiling as if she'd forgotten he'd touched her succulent mouth last night with the pad of his thumb. "We're fine. I told you, Carter. No big deal."

Annoyed that she could shake the interaction so easily, he felt his features draw together. "Cool. What's on the agenda today?"

"After my thrilling breakfast of coffee and eggs, I'll be heading to the Irish pub to watch the Knicks game. You're welcome to join me. I know you love the Knicks." She chucked her eyebrows.

"Sounds like torture, but I'm free, so why not?"

She rolled her eyes. "Glad I'm second place to torture. You know how to make a girl feel special, Carter."

"Sorry," he said, straightening. "I didn't mean to—"

"I'm joking," she said, laughing and grabbing his bicep. "Geez, calm down. Wow, you're really on edge today. It's a holiday. Chill, Carter. You need to relax."

"I woke up in a shit mood. Sorry."

"All good. I'll be there at two. Come over anytime. See ya."

She ambled away, the full globes of her ass almost bursting from her jeans as they strained to contain the flesh. God, he'd love nothing more than to spread her open there and push his cock into her wetness from behind as she cried his name beneath him.

"What the fuck is wrong with you, man?" he asked himself, frustrated that sex with Kayla had suddenly become an obsession. If he wasn't careful, he'd do something stupid and blow their entire arrangement. That would put everything in jeopardy and cause all sorts of questions from their families when Christmas came around if neither of them was with each other.

She deserved better than a guy who was willing to sacrifice everything for a roll in the sack. Determined to do right by her, he headed to shower...and probably jerk off again. Because his dick certainly wasn't as resolved as his brain.

C arter showed up to the pub around two o'clock and took the open seat beside Kayla at the bar. Noticing his forlorn expression, she asked, "You okay? Did the run do you in?"

"Yeah," he said, ordering a scotch from the bartender. "Just got off the phone with Ryan. We're going to spend every weekend with Mom until, well...you know." He sipped the drink and sighed.

"That's good. She'll be happy to have you close by."

He nodded. "I told her I'd spend the weekdays with her too, but she doesn't want me to miss auditions. When she makes up her mind, it's futile to argue with her."

Kayla smiled. "She did seem pretty tough. And I'm sure it's important to her that you continue to live as normally as possible."

"Yeah," he said. "She wants that." The corner of his lips curved and he asked, "How bad are the Knicks losing?"

She punched him in the shoulder. "Hey, they're only losing by four so far." Glancing at the TV that hung above the bar she muttered, "Make that six."

His chuckle surrounded her as he gave her a good-natured jab with his shoulder. Happy that he'd seemed to release a bit of the burden, they proceeded to watch the game. The Knicks lost, of course, and Carter spent the short walk home imploring her to root for another team.

When they reached his apartment, she slipped her arms around him, wanting to comfort him. "Have a good time tomorrow. Enjoy the time with her. It will mean so much when you remember it down the road."

"Thanks," he said, squeezing her before she released him. "I'm really glad you're with me through this, Kayla. I'll be back on Sunday night. Maybe we can hang next week."

Gorgeous irises filled with genuine sentiment stared into her and she found it difficult to catch her breath. "Sure. I'd love that."

Giving her a smile, he entered his apartment.

Once home, she tidied up her place and shot off a few work emails. She contemplated pulling out a steamy romance novel and giving the vibrator a whirl but realized she might never masturbate again. Well, not as long as Carter lived next door and could tease her about it.

As she was falling asleep, she reached back and touched the wall, wondering if he was lying in his bed, only feet from her. Sending him a silent good night, she drifted into slumber.

Chapter 12

K ayla spent Saturday night with Laura and Joy, thrilled to hear
that Laura had gone on a date with Brandon.

"I need to know everything!" Joy exclaimed as they sat at the
table in the Italian restaurant in Chelsea. "And I mean everything!"

Laura laughed and sipped her chianti. "He's super-hot. Like,
off the charts. I love his clear blue eyes, his russet skin and his
smile...well, let's just say that I owe Kayla one."

"Have you guys banged?" Joy asked. "Please tell me that you
banged. I need to live vicariously through you."

"Okay, Miss I'm Never Shaving My Legs Again." Laura joked as
Joy snickered. "We haven't banged yet, but I'm considering it. He's
definitely distracted by this promotion, though. I don't want him
reciting case law in my ear when we finally do it, so I'm going to
wait until your firm makes their choice."

"Should be sometime in mid-December," Kayla said, taking a bite
of her Caesar salad. "I'm ready for them to get it over with too. Did
he mention anything about competing with me? I get the feeling
he's pissed that we're both finalists for the spot."

"No," Laura said, shaking her head, "but he's definitely worried
about it. I can tell—he seems stressed. Hopefully, once Christmas
comes, it will all be gone and we can do the deed."

"Hope so," Kayla said, taking a drink of wine.

"And what about Carter?" Laura asked. "Hmmm? All you told us was that Thanksgiving went well. We need more details. Like, way more. Spill it, sister."

Kayla shrugged. "Not much to tell. We hit it off with both sets of parents and that's what we set out to do. We'll do it again at Christmas and then we'll go back to being neighbors."

"Right," Laura said, eyes narrowing. "I don't buy it for a second. What else happened? I'm just going to keep asking until you tell me, K."

"Nothing," she said, stuffing more salad in her mouth.

"Oh, my god," Joy said. "He tried to kiss you."

Kayla felt her eyes widen and her expression must've given her thoughts away. "No, he didn't," she lied.

Laura's mouth fell open. "Son of a bitch, Joy's right. Spill, Kayla. Now. Or I'll slip a note under his door telling him that you're dying to see his humongous cock and sign your name at the bottom. Swear to god, I'll do it." She crossed an X over her heart.

Kayla rolled her eyes. "Oh, for god's sake. He tried to kiss me, okay?" They both gasped and she gritted her teeth. "His mom is dying and he was seeking comfort. That's all. I put the kibosh on it right away."

"Wait," Joy said, holding up a hand and shaking her head. "You mean to tell me that the hottest guy in Manhattan tried to kiss you and you said no?" Her voice almost ended in a squeak and Kayla told her to shush.

"Yes," she whispered, leaning in since her friends were practically screaming. "He tried to kiss me and I said no. There's no way in hell I'm ever letting him kiss me."

"Why?" Joy asked, as Laura simultaneously yelled, "Why the hell not?"

"Okay," Kayla said, leaning back in her chair and holding up her palms. "You two need to take it down several decibels or I'm done with this conversation. Capiche?"

Their spines straightened and they nodded, appearing to look contrite. Shooting them both glares of warning, she said, "I can't get involved with him romantically, guys. He would decimate me. I'd fall in love with him in a second. Then, he'd get what he wants for a while and he'd leave me in the dust and move on with some chick who's in his league. I just can't."

"I'm so tired of this shit from you, Kayla," Laura said, anger flashing in her hazel eyes. "I've told you that I don't want to hear you put yourself down like that. Your mom is certifiably insane and led you to believe this ridiculous crap about yourself, but it's got to stop. You're the catch, K. Don't you understand? You're out of *his* league."

A laugh burst from Kayla's throat. "Um, yeah, okay."

"It's true, sweetie," Joy said, giving her a caring smile. "You're a kick-ass attorney with an amazing sense of humor and you're absolutely gorgeous. All that thick hair and stunning eyes and your eyelashes...well, my jealousy knows no bounds. He'd be so lucky to be with you."

"Look, I really appreciate you guys saying this stuff. It's not like I think I'm an ogre or anything. But he's also completely incapable of commitment and very upfront about that. I just can't hook up with someone when I know there's not even the possibility of an end game. It's already hard enough for me with my mom chirping in my ear all the time about my weight. I just...I don't know," she said, shaking her head. "To open myself up like that and then have him toss me aside when he's done. I can't set myself up like that. Like you said, I'm smart and I don't pick losing battles."

"Well, *he* tried to kiss *you*, right?" Laura asked. "I mean, he knows exactly what consequences come with that and he tried anyway. Don't you think that he might be open to trying something different with you? You won't know if you don't ask. You're not some bimbo he picked up at a bar. You're the girl he took to meet his mother, for Christ's sakes."

"The *fake* girl in the *fake* relationship," Kayla said.

"You are in no way fake, K," Joy said. "You're, like, the realest person I know."

Kayla breathed a laugh. "You know, Carter said something like that to me too."

A look passed between her friends.

"Okay," Laura said, sitting forward as she ticked items off on her fingers. "First, he tried to kiss you. Second, he made a point of telling you he wasn't faking—"

"That's not exactly what he said—"

"Shhh," Laura interrupted. "Third, he's insanely hot and you have a great time hanging with him. I'm not seeing what the problem is here, honey. You only live once and you need to stop living in fear. You know what? He might break your heart. Shit happens. But he also might realize that you're the best thing that ever happened to him. Joy and I sure have." Kayla felt tears well in her eyes at her friend's tender words. "If you don't even take the chance, you'll never know. I say do it. If he ends up shredding your heart, we'll be here with rocky road and rom-coms. But at least you'll have memories of his magnificent cock."

Kayla laughed, throwing her head back as she gave a groan of frustration. "You guys have no idea what you're urging me to do. It has disaster written all over it."

"Then we'll be here to hug you when you're down, just like Laura said," Joy said, encircling her wrist and squeezing. "You need to take a chance on *some* things in your life, Kayla. Otherwise, what's the damn point?"

Sighing, Kayla shook her head. "I don't know. I'll think about it. That's all I can commit to for now." Grabbing both of their hands, she attempted to blink away the wetness in her eyes, so thankful that she'd found such amazing friends. "I love you guys so much. What would I do without you?"

"Get a lot less cock. That's for damn sure," Laura joked.

Laughing, Kayla shook her head. "I don't really get a lot as it is, but I see your point." Releasing their hands, she lifted her wine and they clinked the crystal together. Smiling into the glass, Kayla said, "So, I didn't tell you guys the best part."

"There's more?" Joy squeaked.

Chuckling, Kayla leaned in, her voice low. "So, the other day, before I met you guys for drinks, I decided I needed a little private time with my vibrator..."

She told them the story, their table devolving into tears of mirth and exclamations of shock. Cherishing every moment with her friends, she thoroughly enjoyed the evening, tucking their words into her subconscious to digest in the days to come.

Chapter 13

♥

Carter spent the weekend at his mom's, Ryan and Patty along with him. Patty asked him several questions about Kayla and he shut her down immediately. Not only was he in a crap mood due to his mom's deteriorating health, but his thoughts always seemed to be stuck on Kayla. And not just thoughts about sex.

Of course, there *were* thoughts of sex. At this point, he'd pretty much imagined being with her in every single position imaginable. Under him, over him, from behind...on the kitchen island, on her comfy couch...hell, even in the stairwell so her boots would clank as he rammed her while she screamed his name in ecstasy. Yep, he had a damn good imagination.

But his thoughts seemed to drift to other things, as well. The way her throat bobbed when she threw her head back and laughed at something he said. Her extreme excitement when she threw her arms above her head and cheered when the Knicks hit a three-pointer. The way she'd hugged him the other day, for no other reason than to give him a moment of comfort. Damn. It had meant so much to him.

"Did you find the records?" Ryan asked, pulling him from his thoughts. They were in his mother's basement, cleaning everything out so it would be ready for her estate sale. The finality of the task was heartbreaking.

"Yeah," Carter said, lifting the dusty box and placing it on a nearby workbench. Flipping through, he noticed some amazing records from bands like Led Zeppelin, Fleetwood Mac and the Doors. "Mom has great taste. These records are awesome."

They spent the next few hours organizing and cataloging and then headed upstairs to hang with Barbara and Dottie. It was a nice weekend and Carter felt some peace since he'd spent some quality time at home.

When Monday rolled around, he attended two auditions and scheduled another one for the next week. Feeling his phone buzz, he answered on the third ring.

"Hey, John."

"Hey, Carter. Got a few minutes?" his agent asked.

"Yep. This must be good. I haven't heard from you in a while." Carter had separate agents for his commercial and theater acting gigs, but he hadn't truly pursued theater in years. The money in commercials was great, if you booked them consistently, and his singing voice was shit. That limited him to only being able to do plays, and most productions wanted more versatile actors.

"There's a play that has a really juicy role and I think you should audition." John detailed him on the part and it sounded pretty fantastic.

"I haven't auditioned for a theater role in three years. I'm pretty rusty."

"Well, I say, brush up on the monologue and get to it. If you don't audition, you'll definitely never get the part."

Basic logic, but true. Nodding, Carter said, "Okay, book it. What's the timeframe?"

"Probably some time in mid-January. I'll keep you posted."

As the phone went dead, he felt a surge of excitement roll through him. Scrolling through his phone, he realized he wanted to tell someone the news. Landing on Kayla's number, he hesitated. Was it weird that she was the first person he wanted to share it with? He could call his brother or one of his buddies, but he had a genuine desire to tell her. Giving in to the notion, he typed the text.

Carter: I have some awesome news. What are you doing tonight?

His heart pounded as the three dots appeared and he wondered why he was so nervous.

Kayla: Really? Sounds juicy. I'm going to be drowning in boring briefs. Send wine.

Carter: Would you want a break? I could certainly show up with wine so you could take an hour.

Kayla: Honestly, I would love to, but I'll be swamped.

Carter frowned.

Kayla: But Wednesday would be good. It will be finalized by then. I'll still be chilling in my PJs on a school night, though. Is that okay?

Visions of her puckered nipple in the barely-there t-shirt from last time filtered through his brain. Yes. That was definitely okay.

Carter: Yep. I can be over at 7. You like cabernet?

Kayla: Sure. Anything red and I'm in. As my friends always say, if I don't have wine teeth, I'm not happy.

Laughing, he typed a reply.

Carter: Sounds sexy. See you Wed.

Kayla: Cool. And congrats on the news. Can't wait to hear!

He sent her an emoji and tucked the phone in his pocket. Excited for Wednesday, and fueled by the upcoming audition, he realized that his mood had improved immensely.

C arter showed up at seven o'clock sharp on Wednesday, and Kayla told the butterflies in her stomach to chill. Ever since the discussion with her friends on Saturday, she'd been toying with the idea of hooking up with Carter. She certainly hadn't made a decision yet and was absolutely terrified of making any sort of move, but it was there...lingering in her mind like a mantra that wouldn't quit.

"Hey," she said, smiling up at him. He looked delicious, dressed in a V-neck gray t-shirt and black sweat pants, athletic slip-ons on his feet. "Come on in."

"You look cute, Summers," he said, setting the wine on the counter and sliding into one of the stools of the island. "I'm glad we can chill and not have to be all formal."

"Me too," she said, using the corkscrew to open the wine and telling herself not to get excited that he thought she looked cute. Cute was definitely not hot or sexy. But, it was something. Pushing the thoughts away, she popped the cork from the bottle. Pouring them two glasses, she set one in front of him and stood across the island, lifting hers high. "To good news," she said.

"To good news." Their glasses clinked and he gave her a sexy smile before drinking.

"So?" she said, "what's the big news? I'm dying to hear."

He told her about his audition and she couldn't help but notice the excitement in his eyes as he spoke. So happy that he had something positive to focus on, she leaned forward, resting her chin on her palm.

"Carter, that's fantastic. I'm so thrilled for you. I really hope you get it."

"It's a long shot, but I'm excited to get out there in the theater world again." His fingers played with the stem of his glass as he seemed to consider his next words.

"What is it?" she asked.

His gaze lifted, those gorgeous melted chocolate eyes latching onto hers. "I..." he shook his head and looked almost...embarrassed? Kayla's eyebrows drew together.

"It was strange," he said, his brow furrowing. "When I got the news, you're the first person I wanted to tell."

Kayla's heart must've shot straight down her spine and out of her body because she'd never felt it slam so hard. Straightening, she gave a smile that she hoped didn't give her thoughts away. The words meant so much to her. "That's awesome. I'm so glad you wanted to tell me." Stunned, she couldn't summon anything else to say.

He stretched his hand across the marble, palm open and waiting. Tentatively, she joined her hand with his. He gently tugged her around the counter, turning so she could walk between his legs. Staring into his eyes, she could barely breathe.

"I keep telling myself that I shouldn't want you. That I'm going to fuck everything up." He slid the pads of his thumbs over the backs of her hands as he stared down at them. "But then you open the door and you smile at me and..." Lifting his gaze to hers, he grinned and gave a slight shrug. "I just melt, Kayla. This is new for me. I don't want to push you or make you feel uncomfortable, and I certainly don't want to mess up our *fake* relationship." He gave a good-natured eye roll at the word. "So, tell me what to do here. I'm leaving it up to you. I think you're attracted to me too, but you seem to have some sort of super-sex-control that I just don't possess. When I want a woman as badly as I want you, I go full force."

"But once you have her you move on," Kayla said, lifting her shoulders before letting them fall. "I'm not worried about the sex. Well, I am, but I'm more worried about what happens after."

"Why would you be worried about the sex?" he asked, eyebrows drawing together.

"Because I'm not a supermodel, Carter. I know your type. They've blazed a trail down our hallway for three years."

His grin was endearing. "Yeah, I've been a player for a long time. I thought it was so great for so long. But, honestly, it's kind of lost its luster."

She shot him a look. "I doubt that."

"It's true," he said, squeezing her hands. "I started spending time with this incredible woman and I kinda lost interest in spending time with anyone else. Go figure."

A deep breath escaped her lungs. "I'm really bad at casual, Carter. It takes a lot for me to sleep with someone. I do want you, but I'm so scared you're going to hurt me."

He nodded, slow and a bit sad. "Honestly? I'm scared of that too. It certainly wouldn't be my intention, but I'm really bad at doing anything but fucking. Sorry to be blunt, but it's true."

A laugh escaped her throat. "I enjoy the bluntness, actually."

Sighing, he swayed their joined hands as he gazed down at them. "I don't know, Summers. I don't want to make you promises I can't keep. You deserve better than that." Lifting his irises to hers, he said, "But I commit to being with you and only you until whatever this is between us runs its course. That's more than I've ever given anyone else, and it should be petrifying, but it's not, and that's why I know it's right."

Lifting her arms, she slid them around his neck. "Well, it's not a line from a Nancy Meyers movie, but you got there anyway."

He grinned, sliding his hands behind her back and drawing her closer. "Is that a rom-com chick thing?"

"Yep," she nodded. "You'd know that if you spent any time actually dating a woman."

"Well," he said, rubbing the tip of his nose against hers, "show me, Summers. I'm open. For you, I'll actually attempt to watch a romantic comedy. Wow. I almost choked on the words."

Laughing, she rested her forehead against his. "It's more than I could ever ask for."

"Fuck, you're so cute. Come here." Pressing his lips to hers, he pulled her close, cementing the silly vow with his kiss.

Kayla's body liquefied, melting into his as she molded herself against him. Opening her mouth, she let him plunder her, his wet tongue sweeping every crevice as moisture gushed between her legs.

Lowering his hands, he cupped the globes of her ass, causing her to moan. As he gently massaged the tender flesh through her thin pants, she felt her knees buckle. He must've sensed her struggle because he lifted her by her ass, gliding her over his thighs so she could wrap her legs around his waist. His erection jutted against her opening, through their clothes, and she thrust her fingers in his hair, purring into his mouth.

Her tongue darted between his lips, searching, tasting, as he breathed her in. Encouraged that he seemed to be struggling for breath as vehemently as she, she writhed over his erection.

"Fuck," he said, breaking the kiss and resting his forehead against hers. "I want to make it good for you, hon. You keep moving like that and I'm going to jizz my pants in about five seconds."

Biting her lip, her eyes locked with his, she pushed her core into his cock.

"You little tease," he said, nipping her lip. "I should've known when I heard you with the vibrator. You're a sex kitten."

Kayla laughed, head thrown back, as he trailed kisses down her neck, causing her to shiver. Never had she felt freer. Being held in Carter's strong arms felt like flying. It might end in disaster, but it was worth it. God, she'd never felt so uninhibited.

"Bed or couch?" she asked, lifting her head to lock gazes with him once more.

"Oh, honey, we're going to fuck on every surface in this apartment. The couch, this counter," he gestured with his head, "the shower. You name it, it's happening. But for tonight, let's start with the bed. I want to see you sprawled out the first time I shove inside you."

Her expression must've fallen because he cupped her cheek. "Hey, where'd you go?"

"I'm here," she said, her throat scratchy.

"Okay, we need to get something straight, Summers." Rubbing his thumb across her lower lip, his gaze was hooded. "You are so damn sexy. Hot as hell with curves for days. I've literally thought about your breasts a billion times. Today." Kayla laughed. "I don't care if you've got flaws. We all do."

She felt her features scrunch as she gave him a sardonic look.

"Yes, even me. Us really, really good-looking people aren't one-hundred percent perfect."

"Are you quoting Zoolander to me?"

"Yes," he said, pecking her on the lips. "I knew you'd get it." His gaze turned reverent as he slid his fingers across her cheek. "You're so beautiful to me, Summers. I need you to believe me. I don't want to do this if you're going to hide yourself from me. You need to trust that I'm insanely attracted to you because it's true."

Inhaling a deep breath, she nodded. "Okay. It's not easy for me to do that, but I'll trust you. You do seem to be pretty turned on right now." She rubbed herself over his cock.

"You're evil, woman." He playfully bit her bottom lip. "Hold on tight."

He lifted to his feet and she yelped, clutching his waist with her legs and his shoulders with a death grip. "I'm too heavy."

"Don't question my manhood," he said, walking to the bedroom, understanding the layout of her apartment since it mimicked his. "I'm the strongest man who's ever lived. You're a feather to me."

"Okay, He-Man," she said, snickering. Stopping at her bedside, he slowly lowered her to the mattress. Feeling the soft comforter at her back, she smiled up at him.

His hands grasped the hem of her shirt, pulling it off in one fell swoop. The cups of her bra were full with her breasts and he crawled over her. Tugging his shirt over his head, he threw it to rest by hers on the floor. Balancing his weight on one hand beside her head, he ran his palm down her neck, between her breasts, eventually cupping one in his hand.

He ran the pad of his thumb over her nipple as it strained through the material, causing her to groan. Pulling the fabric aside, he repeated the action, now skin on skin, causing her to clutch the comforter. "Carter," she pleaded.

"They're just so pretty," he said, seemingly enthralled with her breasts. Lowering his head, he took the straining bud into his mouth.

Kayla's body arched into his, the jolt from his wet tongue sending sparks of desire through her veins. He lavished her, licking and sucking until he gave a frustrated grunt. Reaching behind her, he unclasped the bra, sliding it from her and tossing it to the floor.

Cupping the generous mounds of her breasts in both hands, he devoured her, massaging them as he closed his lips over the other nipple. Kayla writhed below him, her fingers in his hair, the sensation so amazing that she felt tremors deep within.

He gently bit the nub with his teeth, sending her body into overdrive. Calling his name, she jutted her hips into his. His shaft was hard as it pushed against her thigh, almost bruising her, causing her to realize he was as huge as Laura had predicted. Lucky her.

Still lavishing her breast, he glided his hand down, across her abdomen, and slipped it under the hem of her shorts. Searching, his fingers found her small triangle of hair and then slid lower, finding her wet opening.

"Fuck," he moaned against her breast, his finger circling her opening. "You're so fucking wet, Kayla. Holy shit." She relaxed her legs, letting them open, and he took advantage. Eyes locked with hers, he pushed his finger inside.

Her hips moved instinctively, riding his finger as her wetness aided the invasion. "Kayla," his deep voice said, mesmerizing as he played with her. "This is so sexy. Do you always get this wet?"

"Sometimes," she said, feeling slightly embarrassed for some reason. "I don't do this a lot, you know."

He slid over her, leaning his face on his hand as his elbow rested beside her head. "I know. I'm so fucking lucky to be here with you." His eyes searched hers as his finger moved deep within her channel. Adding another finger, he gauged her reaction. "I'm going to make you come so hard."

She bit her lip. "I'm on board with that."

His laugh surrounded her as he lowered his lips to hers. Kissing her thoroughly and deeply, he gathered her wetness on his fingers and slid them up to her clit. As he kissed her, he began rubbing concentric circles over the engorged nub.

"Oh, god," she breathed into his mouth, opening her legs wider to grant him further access.

His tongue continued to assault her mouth as he rubbed her clit, alternating between circles and harder ministrations until his hand was moving at breakneck speed, the sensitized nub beneath drowning in sensation.

"Come on my fingers, Kayla," he commanded, speaking against her lips as she struggled to breathe. His fingers worked her clit, causing her eyes to roll back in her head. "Yes, baby. Come now. You're so close. It's so fucking sexy."

The words snapped something inside her and her body bowed as the orgasm overtook her. Struggling to suck air into her heaving lungs, she clasped onto his biceps, digging her nails into his skin as he hissed above her. He uttered unintelligible words as she focused on the stars exploding behind her closed eyelids. Straining against him, she held on for dear life.

Eventually, the blinding pleasure turned to sated quakes, her body relaxing into a pile of mush underneath his. Lifting her lids, she searched for his eyes, finding them filled with desire and slightly smug.

"Oh, man. Someone's proud of himself," she teased.

His grin was the sexiest thing she'd ever seen. "Oh, I'm just getting started, honey."

"Don't threaten me with a good time—"

She yelped when he lifted her, laughing as he repositioned her, laying her head on the pillow. "Hey, I'm still recovering here."

"No time for recovery, Summers." Inching down her body, he settled between her legs. Shimmying off her pants, he crouched between her legs. Lifting them, he slid one over each of his shoulders. "Open up, honey. I'm going to taste that sweet, wet pussy you've been teasing me with."

A fresh gush of arousal flushed through her heated body. "Oh, god,"

The last thing she saw was his gorgeous smile before he buried his head between her legs.

Chapter 14

♥

C arter was pretty sure he'd died and gone to heaven. Here he was, submerged in Kayla's wet, throbbing pussy, lapping up every drop as she moaned above him. Wanting so badly to please her, he took his time, making sure to use his tongue to swipe across her opening and up to her clit, flicking it several times before he slid back down. Her hands held the comforter in a death grip and he noticed her white knuckles. Good. He wanted her limp and satisfied before he took his own pleasure. That was something that was so easy to give her. She'd given him so much and he ached to give her something in return.

"Are you trying to kill me?" she moaned from the pillow as he speared his tongue inside her wet hole. "Carter, it feels so good. Don't stop."

Chuckling, he sucked one of the folds of her pussy between his lips, then the other, before gliding his tongue up to her clit. Pulling the folds apart with his fingers, he focused on the tiny nub. Tugging the bud between his lips, he sucked, feeling her body tense below him. After drawing her in, he flicked her with the tip of his tongue, loving how her body quaked on the bed.

"Look at me," he commanded, needing to see her stunning eyes as he loved her. They locked on to his, drunk with desire and longing, and he felt like he was home. Gaze glued to hers, he sucked her between his lips again before placing the pads of his fingers on her clit.

"You can do it, baby," he said, gyrating the little nub with his fingers. "Let me get you off one more time before I fuck you." She moaned and he was thankful she seemed to like the dirty words. He always did enjoy a little dirty talk during sex. "Your pussy tastes so good," he said, noticing the flush grow more pronounced across her heated skin. Her breasts hung heavy below her wet, open mouth and he almost came in his pants. She was the most beautiful woman he'd ever seen. Hands down. No contest.

"I'm coming," she cried, head thrown back on the pillow as her body began to shudder. "Oh, Carter, yes!" He continued the strokes on her clit until her legs closed together, her body quaking and trembling upon the bed. Resting his cheek on her thigh, he gazed at her, enthralled with every shake and shiver of her exquisite body.

Her lids slid open, her smile unbearably cute as she stared down at him. "You're really good at that."

Laughing, he nuzzled her thigh with his nose. "Because you taste so damn good. I love licking your pussy, Kayla. We're going to have to do that a lot."

She giggled, the action so adorable that it caused his heart to skip a beat. "I'll allow it." Reaching down, she ran her fingers through his hair. "I think it's time you got some pleasure."

Skillful as a cougar, he slid over her, lowering his lips to hers. "If you think that making you come hasn't given me pleasure, you haven't been paying attention." Thrusting his tongue in her mouth, he gave her a blazing kiss.

Minutes later, he felt his cock might burst if he didn't get it inside her sweet warmth. "Do you have a condom?" he whispered into her mouth.

She nodded, reaching toward the nightstand. Pulling a box from the drawer, she squinted at the side. "Thank god. I thought they might be expired but we're good."

Carter laughed, ripping open the package she handed him. "I have some next door. I didn't bring my wallet with me since I wasn't anticipating this."

He rolled on the condom, loving how she curiously watched him through slitted eyes. Sliding back over her, he aligned their bodies, his eager shaft searching for her opening. Eyes locked with hers, he found it and probed, his ego roaring at her gasp.

"I'm hard as a fucking rock," he said, pushing in slightly. "Tell me if I hurt you."

She nodded, gliding her arms around his neck and holding on for dear life. He jutted into her, inch by inch, teeth gritted as the snug folds of her channel choked him. Engulfed by her swollen walls, he told himself to go slow so she could adjust.

"Good?" he asked when he was buried to the hilt.

"So good," she whispered.

"I'm going to fuck you now, Summers," he said, grinning as he rubbed the tip of his nose with hers. "Relax, okay? It will feel better."

Her body went limp in his arms and his heart swelled that she would allow herself to be so open with him. Pulling his hips back, he withdrew until only the head of his cock remained in her tight pussy. Clenching his teeth, he drove into her.

"Oh, god..." she moaned, digging her nails into his shoulder blades. He loved the sensation and rewarded her with another hard thrust. Energy that he didn't know he possessed surged to his hips and he began fucking her in earnest, balancing the weight of his upper body on his outstretched arms as he pummeled her.

"God, you're so fucking tight, baby," he growled, the muscles of her channel gripping him each time he slid inside.

"Yes," she cried, her head moving on the pillow, hair fanning underneath. Carter thought she looked like a goddess. "It feels so good, Carter."

"Yeah, honey," he said, his hips pistoning into her, plowing her so deeply he thought he might push her through the headboard. Her magnificent tits bobbled up and down as he fucked her. Unable to resist, he lowered and took one of her nipples into his mouth.

She gave a guttural groan and his balls tightened, the orgasm threatening to burst through his straining shaft. Needing to feel her against him when he came, he released her breast and aligned his body with hers. Cupping her shoulder with one hand, he grabbed the generous swell of her ass cheek with the other.

"Look at me," he gritted, heart slamming in his chest when she opened those exquisite eyes. He fucked her mindlessly, their bodies sliding over each other, as she milked him, the sensation overwhelming.

"Kayla," he whispered, spine tingling as his release formed.

Her eyes were bursting with flecks of dark gold within the mahogany. As pleasure shot down his shaft, he had the insane thought that he never wanted to look in anyone's eyes but hers while he was coming ever again. Gripping her shoulder with all his might, he shot into her, emptying himself into her gorgeous body, overcome with shudders.

"Yes," she mewled, clutching him tight as he fell apart in her arms. Burying his face in her neck, he released every drop into the condom, his body bucking with deep spasms. Struggling to suck in air, he relaxed his grip on her ass and shoulder, his body a formless mass of frayed nerves and spent desire. Those sexy-as-fuck nails trailed over his back, tender and lazy, causing him to shiver. There, in her arms, he found heaven.

Barely able to lift his head, he nuzzled her neck. "Holy shit, Summers. You almost killed me."

Her laughter surrounded him, covering his shattered body as she held him close.

Needing to dispose of the condom, he willed his body to move.

"Have. To. Get. Up." He mumbled into her neck.

"No," she whined, her arms tightening around him.

Chuckling, he placed a soft kiss on her neck. "Be right back." With extreme effort, he removed himself from her body, loving how she sluggishly stared at him. Once he'd disposed of the condom, he rolled back into bed, sliding his arm around her waist and drawing her close. She surrounded him, the silky skin of her leg across his thighs, the smooth skin of her cheek on his chest, her palm over his pec.

Wordlessly, he stroked her hair, wishing they could lay there forever. She snuggled closer, wiggling into him and he threaded his fingers through her silken tresses, pulling her tighter. Wrapped in each other's arms, they fell into slumber.

Chapter 15

♥

Kayla awoke to the hushed sounds of Carter dressing. Glancing at the bedside table, she noticed it was almost six a.m., which was when she usually got up for work.

"Hey," he said, pulling his shirt over his head and lowering to the bed. Brushing his fingers through the hair at her temple, he smiled. "I didn't want to wake you."

Kayla wondered what happened now. Did they make plans to hang again? Or to have sex again? How often? The questions were maddening.

"Stop thinking, Summers," he said, trailing his thumb over her cheek. "Don't make it weird."

"I just don't know how to do this," she said, feeling like an idiot. "Do I text you? Do you text me? Do we wait an appropriate amount of time so we don't give the other one the impression that we're dying to see them again?"

He breathed a laugh. "Are you dying to see me again, Summers?"

Realizing it was futile to lie, she whispered, "Yes."

He exhaled a breath, as if he'd been holding it as he waited for her to answer. "Good. Me too. I don't want to play games with you, Kayla. Sex with you was unbelievable. I'd like to do it as often as possible."

She giggled. "I am a self-proclaimed sex kitten."

"You are," he said, giving her a wink.

"I'll be home around six tonight."

"Okay. I'll be home around four. I'll grab dinner and you can just come to my apartment when you're ready."

She nodded, wishing that the world could disappear and she could just curl back into his firm body. But, alas, reality called. "See you around six-thirty."

"Can't wait." He leaned down, securing her lips in a sweet, poignant kiss. "Have a good day, sweetheart." With one last swipe of his thumb across her lower lip, he stood and headed home.

Groaning, Kayla rolled to her back and gave a tiny squeal. She'd had sex with Carter. Wait, scratch that. She'd had *fantastic* sex with Carter. Realizing that she was a little sore down below, she felt her lips curve into a wide smile. Laura would be thrilled to hear that Carter did, indeed, have a magnificently large cock.

Not even attempting to wipe the goofy grin off her face, she plodded to the shower to get ready for work.

C arter had a productive day, most likely spurred along by the perma-grin that had implanted itself on his face. Being with Kayla had been absolutely amazing, and he couldn't wait to see her later. He spent a few hours in the studio recording an audiobook and then headed home to clean his apartment. It wasn't terrible, but he didn't want her to think him a slob.

On the way, he received a text from his buddy Matthew.

Matthew: Hey brother. Long time. Sorry I've been MIA. A few of us are getting together for holiday drinks next Wed. Hope you can make it. McSorley's on 38th at 7.

Carter hadn't hung with Matt in a while and figured he could use a night out with the guys.

Carter: Thanks for the invite. I'll be there.

On the way home, he picked up dinner from one of his favorite Greek restaurants. After cleaning and prepping dinner so it could be heated when Kayla came over, he sat down to practice his monologue. It was from The Departed, which was one of his favorite movies. He practiced for about an hour and noticed it was almost six-thirty. Excitement at seeing Kayla again thrummed in his veins, and he told himself to calm down.

A knock sounded at his door, and there she stood, with that brilliant smile, knocking the wind from his lungs.

"I found a nice bottle of scotch at the liquor store on the way home," she said, shaking it in her hand. "Figured you could show me how to drink it."

"Lady, you're speaking my language."

Laughing, she sauntered in and set it on the counter. Turning to face him, he noticed how nervous she looked. Thank goodness. It made him feel better since his heart was pounding like a lovesick fool.

"Did you miss me?" he asked, inching toward her until their bodies brushed.

"Yes," she whispered.

Cupping her face, he tilted her head back. "Show me." Lowering his lips to hers, he breathed her in, sucking her tongue into his mouth. Extending his wet tongue, it warred with hers, battling in a clash where they both won. The sexy purrs she shot down his throat made a beeline to his shaft and he lowered his hands to cup her ass. Lifting her, he sat her on the island, loving her high-pitched squeak at the sudden movement.

He tore the shirt from her body, fisting his hand in her hair to draw her head back, exposing the luscious skin of her neck to his lips. She tasted like spring and heaven and sweetness, all rolled into the woman that was Kayla.

Her scattered moans shattered his control and he gripped the waistband of her thin pajama pants, awkwardly pulling them down her legs until they fell to the floor. Sliding her toward him, he seated his erection in the juncture of her thighs. Staring into her deep brown eyes, he said, "I need to fuck you. *Now*."

She nodded, encircling his neck with her arms. With shaking hands, he grabbed his wallet on the counter and pulled out a condom. After shucking his pants to his knees, he slid the condom on. Hooking his fingers around the thin cloth that covered her opening, he drew it aside.

"I'm going to fuck you around these cute little panties," he growled. Aligning his tip to her opening, she wiggled against him, driving him insane.

"Please," she whimpered.

Cupping her hips, he impaled her, loving how she clutched his shoulders. Her head fell back as he began jutting into her, his hips barreling at a pace that had him gasping.

Looking between their straining bodies, he watched his dick move in and out of her pussy, the pretty pink underwear still pushed to the side, the image hot as hell. Every time his cock withdrew and reentered her, he felt like he was claiming her. *Mine*, his brain screamed. He wanted to own every inch of her gorgeous body.

Arching her back, she rested her palms on the marble, allowing her legs to open wider. The deeper access meant her tight channel could take more of him and he took advantage, pushing so deep inside, he thought she might swallow him whole.

"This is all I could think about today," he said, the sound of his balls slapping against her ass each time he impaled her driving him wild. The room smelled of sex and desire, and he reveled in how exquisite she was atop the staid counter.

"Me too," she cried, head falling back as he undulated his hips, searching for a spot deep within that would make her crazy.

"Can you come from this?" he asked, understanding that some women only came from clitoral stimulation.

"If you hit the right—oh, yes!" Her body bowed and he focused on hitting the exact spot where he'd been when she tightened. "Right there...don't stop."

"No way, baby," he said, working his hips to jut the head of his cock toward the right place, wanting so badly to please her. Her body quaked beneath him and he felt her tightening, bit by glorious bit, knowing she was on the precipice of coming.

Concentrating with all his might, he pummeled her, feeling his knees buckle from the intense pleasure of her tight walls milking him. Suddenly, she broke, body arching toward his, and screamed his name as she began bucking against him. Pulling her hips to his with the firm grip of his hands, he battered their bodies together, feeling his own climax on the horizon.

The walls of her pussy undulated against him, clamping around him in a pulsating vice. Unable to take the intense pleasure, he let go, spurting his release as he emitted a wail so loud it could probably be heard down the block at the pub.

He collapsed over her, his muscles turning to jelly, as his hips quaked, gushing his release. Breathless and panting, he precariously balanced on his shaking arms.

"Holy shit, Kayla," he said, "what did you do to me?"

She groaned, sated and sexy, and he struggled not to collapse in a pool of sated arousal on the floor. He felt her pussy clench around his over-sensitive cock and lifted his head to look into her eyes. "You witch," he said, pecking her on the lips. "You're squeezing me."

White teeth bit her swollen bottom lip. "Does it feel good?"

"Everything you do to me feels good, honey." Pressing his lips to hers, he devoured her mouth, sweeping the depths with his tongue. "I swear, you're a sex master. If I had only known this three years ago. Talk about wasted time."

She giggled, so adorable as she grinned up at him. "Let me get rid of the condom." He pulled out of her, enthralled by the wetness that shined on his cock. It was so damn sexy that she got so wet for him. He ambled to the bathroom, difficult since his pants were still around his legs, but managed to make it. When he returned, she was wearing her pants and reaching for her shirt.

"Leave it off," he said, grabbing the shirt and placing it on one of the kitchen stools. "We'll have shirtless dinner, but you can leave the bra on." He gave her a wink.

Her gaze lowered as she contemplated. Carter took the moment to study her. Her skin was smooth and luscious. Her belly wasn't flat where it met the waistband of her pants. Instead, it was flared with curves and ridges that seemed to go on for days. Stepping toward her, he gently placed his palm on her belly.

"You're so gorgeous, Kayla. I like looking at you."

Cavernous brown eyes stared into his. "I have rolls, Carter. Like, legit rolls."

He trailed his hand over her stomach, stopping at one of the gentle curves that hung slightly over the waistband at her side. "This?" he asked, skimming his fingers over her silky skin. "This is so sexy, Summers. It's the first part of you I was attracted to."

Her eyebrows drew together. "What?"

"When I came over to plan our fake dating origin story. You reached up to grab some plates and this," he swiped his fingers over the skin, "peeked back at me. My dick grew hard immediately. It's so hot, Kayla."

"No way," she said.

"Yep. And then, I got stuck on your toes." He glanced down at her feet. "I'm going to have to play with those later."

"I didn't peg you for a toe fetish guy."

"I wasn't until I met you." Leaning down, he brushed a kiss across her lips. "There were a lot of things I didn't realize until I started hanging with you. Leave the shirt off, Summers. I want to see your gorgeous breasts burst from that thin-as-hell bra while you're in my house. Please?"

"Fine," she said, rolling her eyes. "But if you're grossed out, just remember I warned you."

"Um, hi," he said, giving her a sardonic look. "If I'm ever grossed out by a sultry half-naked woman, please get me to an infirmary immediately."

She laughed and glanced toward the food on the back counter. "Want to heat up dinner?"

"Let's do it."

They prepared the assortment of gyros, hummus and Greek salad and settled on his couch to eat. Carter turned on the Knicks game, and they sat in comfortable silence. Her adorable toes, now painted purple, rested near his thigh and he reached down, pulling her feet to rest against his leg. She smiled, chewing, and snuggled further into the couch as her feet pushed against him.

So, this was what being in a relationship was like. Huh. Carter studied her out of the corner of his eye as he ate. He'd always assumed relationships were cold and devoid of passion. When he was still young, and his parents were together, he'd noticed nothing but coldness and mistrust between them. Their toxic energy had permeated their home until Carter's father eventually left, never to return. He never blamed his mom—she raised him and Ryan, after all—but always thought his dad was the worst piece of shit for leaving her with two kids.

As far as he knew, they never spoke again. Barbara didn't take alimony or child support and worked her entire life as a nurse to pay the bills. Thank goodness for Dottie, who had always been there, watching over them when his mom was at work. The entire mess had turned him off of relationships completely. Why waste time cultivating something that was ultimately doomed to fail? The divorce rate in Manhattan was inexorably high. Many of his friends had already been divorced, some of them twice. Carter just didn't see the logic of tying himself to one person forever.

After all, people changed, didn't they? Life evolved and people's tastes along with it. Many of his married friends complained that they never had sex with their wives, especially after having kids. That sounded like torture to Carter. Why set yourself up for that? There were so many beautiful, unattached women in the city to have fantastic sex with. Why sign up for one woman for the rest of your life?

Chewing thoughtfully, he thought about Ryan. He seemed happy with Patty and they'd been married for several years. Deciding that he needed to grill his brother about the subject, he glanced at Kayla, noticing her studying him.

"What are you thinking about over there?" she asked, pushing her feet into his thigh. "You look super serious."

He smiled. "I was thinking that I need to pour us some scotch."

"Ohhhh," she said, eyes sparkling. "Let's do it. Not too much, though, because I have to work tomorrow."

He stood, reaching over to grab her now-empty plate, and took them both to the sink. Returning with two tumblers of scotch, he sat beside her, placing his arm around her shoulders and drawing her into his side.

"Okay, the first thing you need to do is bring the glass to your nose and inhale with your mouth open." He watched her, marveling at her open mouth, dying to get those full lips around his cock sooner rather than later. "Now what?" she asked, staring up at him.

Her upturned face was so adorable that he had to steal a kiss. Leaning back, he said, "Now you drink. Slowly, so that it doesn't shock your system."

She lifted the tumbler to her lips, eyes locked with his, slowly drinking. When in the hell did drinking scotch become a certified sex act? He wasn't sure but watching Kayla drink the brown liquid did all sorts of things to his cock. She swallowed, her throat bobbing, and smiled. "It's good."

Nodding, he took a sip, reveling in the slight burn and smooth taste. Settling in, he raised the volume on the TV, loving how she snuggled into his side. Her warm skin pressed against his and she rested her head at the juncture of his shoulder and chest. His fingers trailed gently along the smooth skin of her side, reveling in the tiny bumps that arose.

When his glass was empty, he gazed down at Kayla. She was asleep, her mouth slightly open, the forgotten scotch in her hand. Something profound washed over him as he realized how lucky he was that she trusted him enough to fall asleep in his arms. It was so precious and he vowed not to squander it.

"Hey, hon," he said, slightly shaking her. "The game's over. Time to go to sleep."

"Oh," she said, straightening and rubbing her eye. "Crap. Why do I always fall asleep on you?"

"It's fine. I like watching you sleep. You look so peaceful."

She looked to the ceiling, her expression playfully contemplative. "I can't decide if that's creepy..."

Laughing, he took her glass and rose, padding over to deposit both in the sink. When he turned around, she was putting on her shirt. Bummer.

"I'm going to head home, brush my teeth and go to bed," she said, hesitant as she stood before him. "As much as I would love another bout of sex, I'm beat, and I don't want to overstay my welcome."

Carter swallowed, overcome with sadness at her departure. He wanted her to stay, even if they didn't have sex. Holy shit. That had never happened with a chick before. But he felt it, deep in his bones—the desire to hold her against his body as they both drifted to sleep. It was...terrifying. Unable to process it, he nodded. "Okay. Good night. Sweet dreams, Summers."

Smiling, she approached him. Lifting to her toes, she gave him a soft kiss. "Night, Carter."

As he watched her amazing ass sway out the door, he cursed himself a fool. After cleaning up and brushing his teeth, he slipped into bed, aching for the warmth of her body. Lifting his hand, he touched the wall, wondering if she was there. Wishing he wasn't such a coward, he sent her wishes of sweet dreams and rolled over to get some sleep.

Chapter 16

♥

K ayla smiled when Carter's text lit up her phone.

Carter: So, I think it's time I take you on a date. Tonight. Dinner @ Sofia Wine Bar. Pick you up at your door at 7.

Kayla: That's very presumptuous, Mr. Manheim. I might already have plans.

Carter: No way. How could you pass up the opportunity to have wine, dinner and sex with your favorite neighbor? Did I mention there will be sex afterward? Come on, Summers.

Chuckling, she worked her thumbs over the keypad.

Kayla: You're lucky because Laura has a date and Joy's sister is in town. Is the place fancy?

Carter: Fancy enough for those sexy boots. Wear them with a skirt, but no hose, okay? As soon as we get home, I'm going to ravish you while you're still in the boots.

A gush of moisture rushed between her thighs and she bit her lip.

Kayla: I feel like you've thought about this a few times already.

Carter: Honey, if you knew how many times I've imagined fucking you in those boots, you'd probably have me arrested. See you at seven.

She smiled and looked around the office, wondering if anyone could see what a sap she was being. Everyone seemed hard at work and oblivious. Thank goodness.

Kayla: K. See you then.

She put the phone down and lifted it again when it buzzed.

Carter: PS—I've thought about you all day. Miss you. See you later.

Kayla's heart pounded so hard she thought it might shoot from her chest. Feeling like a sappy idiot, she hummed as she resumed typing the oral argument she was preparing for her boss.

That evening, she showered and spent extra time putting on her makeup. Although she'd never been a big fan of the stuff, she wanted to look extra pretty for Carter. Dressing in a black sweater dress and a matching black thong and bra, she zipped the boots to her knees. Staring at her reflection, she ran her hand over her hair, which was thick and wavy. Her eyes looked exotic, thanks to the eyeliner she'd applied, and she felt attractive. Sexy, even. It was a rare feeling and she relished it, realizing that she had Carter to thank. He truly seemed to love her curves, much to her surprise. It was a welcome boost to her always fluctuating self-esteem.

Pulse quickening when she heard the knock on the front door, she rushed to it, pulling it open. Carter's eyes seemed to bug out of his head.

"Holy shit, Summers," he said, shaking his head. "We have reservations. How can you open the door looking like that?"

"What?" she asked, suddenly worried she'd applied too much makeup, or maybe the sweater dress made her look fat.

"You little tease," he said, closing in and snaking an arm around her waist. Drawing her against his body, he murmured against his lips, "How am I supposed to stop myself from fucking you right here? You look *incredible*." He enveloped her in a slow, torturous kiss. "Good grief," he said, resting his forehead against hers. "The things you do to my heart, Summers." Placing a peck on her lips, he stepped back slightly.

"Okay, we have to go." Releasing her, he shook his head. "Dinner, Carter. Dinner," he mumbled to himself. Extending his hand, he lifted his brows. "Well, come on, hon. If you don't leave with me now, I'm not responsible for what happens."

Thrilled at his response to her appearance, since she'd taken so much time to make it perfect, she latched onto his hand and let him lead the way.

The restaurant was a few blocks away and they were seated at the window. They ordered wine and a charcuterie plate to start, and Kayla laughed when he tried to feed her cheese.

"Stop it," she said, swatting his hand. "I'm perfectly capable of feeding myself." Grabbing a chunk of brie, she tossed it in her mouth and began chewing. "Mmmm..."

Smiling, he took a sip of wine. "I have something I'd like to feed you later."

The laugh burst from her lips. "Wow. No subtlety there. A master of words, you are not, Carter."

"What?" he asked, shrugging. "I was talking about the Greek leftovers."

Rolling her eyes, she chuckled. "You were talking about your..." she tilted her head toward his lap, "*you know*. I'm not an idiot."

Sitting back, he lifted his hands. "If you can't resist sucking me, I'll have to let you, Summers. It sounds scandalous, but you are a certified sex goddess."

"Shhh..." she said, glancing around to see if anyone heard him. Fortunately, the restaurant was loud and everyone was deep in their own conversations.

He leaned forward, pressing his lips to her ear. "Don't worry, honey. I'll be gentle. I can't wait to see those gorgeous lips around my cock. I might even pull your hair while you suck me if you're a good girl."

She pushed him away, her body hot and wet from his teasing. "Stop it, Carter."

"Are you wet?" he murmured.

"Yes," she whispered.

"Fuck," he breathed. "Okay, I'm stopping. Otherwise, I'm going to make a mess at the table."

She laughed, taking a sip of her wine as she felt the slickness inside her thong. Realizing that she'd never felt such intense attraction for someone, she allowed herself to enjoy it. Carter was probably the hottest guy she would ever be with, and for some reason still elusive to her, he was insanely attracted to her too. It was unbelievable and so damn exciting.

The waiter brought the main dishes and they caught up on life. Carter's expression grew somber when he updated her on his mom's funeral arrangements, which he and Ryan were planning.

"She wants you to come visit on Sunday," he said, irises searching hers, filled with a bit of hesitation. "I told her I'd ask you, but don't feel obligated. I'm heading out tomorrow morning. Dottie's cooking on Sunday and Mom mentioned that she'd love to have you there. She obviously doesn't realize our relationship is fake."

The words hurt, even though she knew he didn't mean them to, and his eyebrows drew together. "That didn't come out right. I, uh...you know what I mean, right?"

Kayla nodded, reminding herself that their relationship was, indeed, fake. Just because they were having sex, that in no way meant they were a couple.

"Damnit, Kayla," he said, gripping her hand. "I didn't mean to hurt your feelings. I was just talking about our arrangement—"

"It's fine," she interrupted, squeezing his hand. "I know what you meant. I'd love to come on Sunday."

"Yeah?" he asked, his smile hesitant.

"Yeah. I'll Uber out. Just text me the address."

"Thank you," he said, lifting her hand to place a kiss on her knuckles. "She's so excited that I finally have a girlfriend for once in my life. I don't have the heart to tell her...well, I just want her to be happy."

He didn't have the heart to tell her it wasn't real. Kayla's heart shattered into a thousand pieces as her mind completed the sentence he was too polite to speak aloud. None of it was real to him. Swallowing thickly, she lowered her gaze, telling herself to buck up and push the tears away STAT. She was a big girl and she knew *exactly* what she'd signed up for with Carter. This shouldn't be a shock or a surprise. Inhaling a deep breath, she took a sip of wine.

"I'm looking forward to it. I like spending time with your family." Pasting on a smile, she trudged through the dinner, determined not to indicate that her heart was broken inside her chest.

C arter held Kayla's hand as he walked beside her, cursing himself for the terrible way he'd handled the conversation about this weekend's visit. He'd only meant to make clear that Kayla shouldn't feel obligated to extend their fake relationship beyond the agreed-upon holidays. Instead, the words had come out all wrong and he could tell she was hurting. Wishing he wasn't such an idiot, he squeezed her hand.

"So, what's on the agenda tomorrow?"

"I'm hanging with the girls. We always do a holiday shopping day filled with many stops for food and wine along the way."

"Nice," he said, leading her up the stairs to their building and holding the door. "Sounds fun."

"It is," she said, her tone devoid of emotion. Fuck. She was really hurting. He felt like a bona fide asshole.

When they reached his door, she pointed to hers. "Your place or mine?"

"Yours," he said, leading her there, hoping that would help her feel more on solid ground. When they entered, she took off her coat and faced him. "So, bed or couch?"

"Wait," he said, eyeing her. Removing his coat, he hung it on the rack beside her door. Slowly closing the distance between them, he searched her gorgeous face. He had no idea what she'd done with her makeup tonight, but she was spectacular. "I didn't mean to hurt you, Kayla. I'm sorry."

She shrugged. "I'm fine. We made a decision to have sex, so let's have sex. I'm ready. Do you want me to take off my dress?"

"Stop," he said, grabbing her wrists and drawing her to him. "Just stop, Summers. You're trying to make this all about sex and it's not. Stop twisting my words."

"You've been nothing but clear that this is a fake holiday relationship and that we just added sex to the mix. I'm an adult, Carter. I know what this is. I'm not mad."

Right. She was pissed, but he wanted to tread lightly.

He breathed a heavy sigh. "I struggle with how to define this, Kayla. I don't want you to feel obligated to visit my mom outside of the confines of what we agreed upon. That's all. I have no claim over you. I just wanted to make that clear."

She nodded. "Crystal clear. Got it."

Frustration surged through him at her tone. "You're obviously pissed at me. I'm not a mind reader. Just get it out, Kayla. Tell me I'm an asshole or whatever the hell you want to tell me. Because I was having a really nice time with you tonight and now it's gone to shit."

"Yes, sorry to have ruined your sure thing," she said, rolling her eyes. "I know how unacceptable it is for you not to get laid on a Friday night." Wrenching from his grasp, she backed away. "I think it's best if we just cool off tonight. Sorry, Carter. I'm just not feeling it. You can show yourself out."

Pivoting, she stalked to her room and closed the door. Annoyed at the turn of events, Carter rubbed his eyes with his fingers, giving a loud groan.

Thinking back on their conversation, he tried to remember exactly what he'd said. He'd told her that she shouldn't feel obligated...because their relationship wasn't...*real*. Fuck. He'd actually indicated that he felt that way, even if he hadn't said the actual word. Feeling like the biggest ass in the world, he walked to her bedroom door and lightly rapped his fingers on the surface. Hearing her quiet sobs, his heart splintered in his chest. Pushing open the door, he saw her lying on the bed, back facing the door, curled into a ball hugging a pillow.

Slowly sitting on the bed, he laid a gentle hand on her shoulder. "Kayla," he said, the pain from the knowledge that he'd made her cry almost crippling. "Please, honey, let me make this right. I'm so sorry. I told you I suck at this. Please don't cry, baby."

Urging her to turn over, his breath caught at the genuine emotion in her wet eyes. Stretching out beside her, he cupped her cheek. "I'm sorry, hon. I told you I was going to fuck this up."

"You said it isn't real," she warbled, her eyes pleading with his. "How could you say that? Every moment I'm with you is so fucking real, Carter. How can you feel nothing?"

"Sweetheart," he said, the organ crumbling in his chest proving her words a lie. "I was trying not to burden you. I don't want you to feel obligated to me. That's all, I swear." Lifting her hand, he held it to his heart. "Do you feel this? It's so fucking real. Every time I'm with you, Kayla. It scares the shit out of me. I don't know what it is, but it sure as hell is real as fuck."

"I have feelings for you, Carter. I know that's hard for you to digest, but I don't want to lie to you."

The words sent shivers of pleasure over his body. "I'm so honored that you do. It's such a gift, honey. Please, let me love you in the way that I can. I want to hold you."

Her eyes searched his and, eventually, she nodded. Reaching for him, she encircled his neck and he pressed his lips to hers. "I don't know how to show you, hon," he breathed into her mouth. Lathering her with his tongue, he tasted the essence of his beautiful Kayla. "All I can give you is this."

She surged against him, thrusting her tongue in his mouth, consuming him as he burned for her. Sliding his hand under her dress, he found her core and inserted his finger into her wetness.

"Yes," she moaned, undulating to meet him.

Ravaged by desire, he shifted her, sitting her up so he could pull the dress from her body. She reached back to unhook her bra while he tore at his clothes. When she reached down to pull off her thong, he grabbed her hands, halting her.

"Look at you," he said, desire thrumming through his frame. "Stay right there."

Straightening, he ripped off the remainder of his clothes, throwing them to the floor. Opening her bedside table drawer, he pulled out the condoms and rolled one on his straining shaft. Returning to her, he grabbed each of her boot covered ankles, pulling her to the edge of the bed so she straddled him. Hooking his hands beneath her underwear, he slid it over her boots and tossed it to the ground.

Grasping both of her ankles, he lifted them high in the air, resting them on his shoulders. She was spread open below him, her pussy glistening in the light of the dim lamp by her bedside, her breasts large and supple below her stunning face.

Lowering his hand to her core, he cupped her, inserting a finger in her wetness and lifting it to his mouth. Eyes locked with hers, he licked her sweet essence from his own skin. She mewled, her swollen eyes filled with desire and emotion.

Gripping her ankles at his shoulders, he lined the head of his cock with her opening. Gaze cemented to hers, he began to push in. His hips undulated as she writhed upon the bed, biting her sexy-as-sin lip as he fucked her. Holding the faux leather tight, he worked her pussy until it was glistening.

"It's like a fucking dream, Kayla," he said, overcome with lust at her boot-clad legs and pale, quivering body. "All I dream about is fucking you in these sexy boots. God, honey, you're everything I've ever wanted. Don't you know that?"

"Carter," she cried, eyes closing as she gyrated below him.

Moving his thumb to her clit, he began to stimulate it as he thrust into her. She cried out as he rubbed, needing to give her pleasure as her tight channel choked his straining cock. The sight of his shaft, sliding through her silken wetness, below the tiny black hairs of her mound, was *everything*. Loving how responsive she was, he vowed to make her scream.

Increasing the pace of his thrusts, he continued the motion of his thumb.

"This is so real, Kayla," he said through gritted teeth. "Right here. Just you and me. Take it, baby." She groaned below him, hair fanning behind her as he jutted into her. "God, you're so beautiful."

Feeling his knees grow weak, he collapsed over her, clutching her shoulders as he fucked her, deep and raw. Her leather-clad legs locked behind his back and he growled in ecstasy.

"Don't let me push you away," he growled in her ear. "I need you, Kayla. So fucking much." Groaning, he felt his balls tense and a tingling at the base of his spine. Her nails dug into his scalp, pulling his hair, and he bit the lobe of her ear, causing her body to buck beneath him.

Face buried in his neck, she spoke words of love and desire, and he clutched onto them, needing them as desperately as the air he breathed. His body bowed and he came, emptying himself into her as she cried his name beneath his shattered frame. Feelings of such depth swamped him as he shuddered inside her, ones he couldn't name but knew they were profound. Clutching her, he relaxed into her supple body, understanding that something had shifted in their relationship tonight. Unable to process it, he held her, needing to feel her warmth.

Eventually, she tapped his shoulder and he lifted his head. Grinning, he gave her a peck on the lips. "Am I crushing you?"

"Yeah," she said, giving him that adorable smile.

"Don't move," he murmured against her lips. "I want to be the one who unzips those sexy boots tonight."

She nodded and he headed to the bathroom, his limbs shaky and unsure. Not just from the amazing sex, but from the knowledge that they'd far surpassed the fuck-buddy stage. Kayla was in deep—he'd seen the emotion in her eyes as he'd fucked her. And, honestly, he was in deep too. He wasn't sure how deep, but it was somewhere between complicated and really fucking complicated. Sighing, he disposed of the condom and headed back to her room.

Silent, he lifted her leg, sliding the zipper down, baring her soft skin. Trailing kisses along each inch of exposed skin, he removed the boot and repeated the same on her other leg. When she was lying deliciously naked before him, he slid onto the mattress and gathered her in his arms.

She laid her cheek on his chest and he stroked her hair as he contemplated.

"This isn't fake anymore," he said, placing a kiss on the crown of her head.

"It isn't for me," she murmured against his chest.

"Fuck," he whispered, pulling her close.

"I'm so tired," she warbled against his chest.

"Go to sleep, sweetheart. I'll be here when you wake up." Caressing her with his strong hands, he reveled in the softening of her breathing as she relaxed into his sated body.

Chapter 17

♥

Kayla awoke to Carter's firm heartbeat beneath her ear. Snuggling into him, she placed a kiss on his chest. Exploring, she noticed the scratchy hairs that narrowed to a V and his chiseled eight-pack.

"Admiring the merchandise, Summers?" he teased above her.

"Yep," she said, nodding. "How do you maintain these abs?"

"A hell of a lot of crunches. If you hear me grunting next door, I'm either doing those or imagining you with the vibrator, if you know what I mean."

Laughing, she rested her chin on her hand, elbow leaning on his chest. "What time are you leaving to go to your mom's?"

He picked up his phone from her nightstand, noting the time. "In about an hour. I told her I'd get there early, to do some yard work since winter's coming. Then, Ry and I will go work out. Then dinner." Running his fingers over her cheek, he said, "And then tomorrow, I'll see you."

She nodded. "I'm excited to see your mom again. And Ryan and Patty. She's awesome. Your brother snagged a good one."

"He did."

"Are we okay?" she asked, feeling like a dolt for breaking down in tears last night. "I acted like an annoying girlfriend last night, and I know that's the last thing you want or need. I hope I didn't scare you off."

His brown irises darted between hers. "At this point, Summers, you might as well be my girlfriend. I find myself wanting to spend every second I can with you. When I'm not with you, I think about the next time I'll be with you. What the hell have you done to me?"

Elation coursed through her at his words. "I feel the same," she whispered.

"Do you know that you're the first woman I've ever slept with?"

She arched a sardonic brow.

Chuckling, he ran his fingers through her hair. "I mean through the night. I've done it twice now. And I wanted to ask you to stay on Thursday, but I chickened out."

"You did?"

He nodded.

"Well, I'm quitting while I'm ahead. It's more than I ever expected from our *arrangement*." She waggled her eyebrows. "I'll do my best not to push you, Carter. I want this to happen naturally. I think we're great together."

"Me too," he murmured. "And you know what else I think?"

She bit her lip and shook her head.

"I think I need to fuck you again before I go home."

"Is that so?" she asked, sliding her leg up and down his hairy one. "We don't have much time—"

She squeaked as he rolled her over, quick as lightning, and dug his erection into her thigh. "Good thing I'm ready for you," he growled, burying his face in her neck and kissing a wet trail along her pulsing vein.

Throwing her head back, Kayla let him show her how ready he truly was as she gave in to the pleasure of his skillful caresses.

K ayla had a fantastic day shopping with Laura and Joy. Of course, when she told them she and Carter were sleeping together, she thought their eyes might literally pop from their sockets.

"Oh, my god, Kayla!" Joy exclaimed as they sipped the hot chocolate they'd purchased from a street vendor at one of the tables in the city park. "I'm so proud you took the leap! How's the sex?"

"More importantly, how big is his cock?" Laura asked, waggling her eyebrows.

"It's amazing and...well, it's amazing," Kayla said, snickering.

They all giggled like teenagers as they reveled in Kayla's happiness.

"You're glowing, K," Laura said. "Good for you."

"I almost blew it last night." Kayla told them the story about Carter's categorization of their relationship at dinner and her subsequent meltdown. "He told me not to let him push me away. I think he has feelings for me but he's terrified of them."

"Why?" Joy asked.

Kayla shrugged. "I think it's because his dad left when he was young. I'm going to try and ask Patty tomorrow if I can get her alone. She's hella cool."

"Well, it seems like he's trying," Laura said. "I mean, he's acting like a boyfriend. I think you're right to just let things evolve naturally. Hopefully, it will all work out."

"I hope so," Kayla muttered.

The next day, she called a rideshare to New Jersey, arriving at Barbara's house around noon. They sat in the living room listening to Barbara's old records and sharing memories of her life. She'd been a nurse for thirty years and had such colorful stories.

They sat down to dinner around five o'clock and Carter reached over to grab her hand and squeeze it. "Thanks for being here," he whispered.

"Sure," Kayla said, squeezing back.

Dottie prepared yet another scrumptious meal and they all were in a food coma by seven o'clock. Carter had rented a Zipcar for the weekend and he drove them back while Kayla sang along to the Christmas tunes on the radio.

"Who knew you liked Christmas songs, Summers? You have a nice voice."

"Thanks," she said, beaming. "I used to love to sing in chorus in high school."

They belted out the tunes until they returned to their apartment. Once they reached their floor, Carter took her hands.

"I know you have to work tomorrow and I'm tired. I'd really like you to stay with me, but it doesn't have to be sexual. If you want to just sleep together, I'm fine with that."

Kayla studied him, realizing this was probably the first time he'd ever made such an offer to a woman. It might not seem like much but was most likely profound to him. "Let me brush my teeth and wash my face and I'll come over, okay?"

He nodded, looking relieved as if he thought she'd say no for some reason.

After prepping for bed, she threw on her nicest pair of satiny sleep shorts and a soft tank over a thin bra. Throwing on a robe, she headed next door.

He'd left the door open for her and she closed it behind her, turning the deadbolt. Padding to his room, she found him lying in bed, scrolling through his phone.

"Hey," he said, placing the phone on the nightstand. "Come on in." He swept back the covers.

Feeling shy, she grasped the robe and shrugged it off, tossing it on the chair beside his bed. Climbing into bed with him, she felt him reach over her and turn off the lamp. Drawing her back into his front, he spooned her, his warm breath at her neck. Kayla could feel his erection jutting into the crease of her butt.

"I'm open to having sex if you want," she said, yawning as she finished the sentence.

He kissed her neck. "It will go down eventually. I'm tired too. And, honestly, it was hard seeing Mom so thin today. I'm mentally exhausted."

"I'm here for you," she said, trailing her nails back and forth over the hairy skin of his arm. "Always, Carter. Whatever you need."

"I need to hold you," he murmured, hugging her so tight that she felt they were breathing the same air. It was magnificent. She stroked him, long and lazy until her eyes drooped and his breaths slowed to a long, steady pace.

"I would let you hold me forever, Carter," she whispered, her heart pounding as she waited to hear his response. His soft snore reverberated in her ear and she smiled, thankful he hadn't heard the words. But she'd said them and they were true. Realizing she was in too deep to save herself, she gave up trying. Giving into exhaustion, she fell asleep in his warm embrace.

Chapter 18

♥

The next week dragged along as Carter immersed himself in various projects. Kayla was working on a brief that required extra hours, so he barely saw her. They met up to share a quick meal in his apartment on Tuesday night, but she headed back to her own apartment, telling him she was drained. He kissed her mindlessly, needing her to know how much he would miss having her soft body next to his as he slept.

It was amazing that, after thirty-five years on the planet, he'd finally met someone that he wanted to spend every day and every night with. Carter had never had the urge to cuddle with anyone, but he actually *craved* the feel of Kayla's body against his. It wasn't just the silken texture of her skin, although that was a resplendent bonus, but it was the way she snuggled into him. It relied a trust and openness that he'd never felt with anyone and he was becoming addicted to it.

On Wednesday, he went to meet Matt and a few other friends for drinks. A few rounds in, Matt slapped him on the shoulder.

"So, you're still single right?" Matt asked.

Carter felt his eyebrows draw together. *Technically*, he was still single, since he and Kayla hadn't labeled their relationship, but he had promised to only be with her until their time together ran its course. "I'm in a monogamous relationship with someone right now," he said, the words sounding strange on his tongue.

"No shit, man?" Matt asked. "You? Wow, I thought you'd pledged to be single forever."

Carter laughed, feeling uncomfortable. "I'm certainly not dying to get married, but she's a great girl and I like her a lot."

Matt nodded. "Good for you, man. I'm happy for you."

Later that evening, as he walked home, Carter contemplated their conversation. Where was this thing with Kayla going? Did he want to make a commitment to her? Move in with her? Marry her? The thoughts seemed daunting and he had trouble reconciling them.

Carter had never wanted to get married, but Kayla seemed like the type of girl who wanted that. Did she want kids? They'd never talked about it. Although he liked Kayla a lot and didn't want to be with anyone else, he also owed it to her to be honest about what he wanted in the future.

Deciding that he didn't want to mess up their arrangement, he concluded that he would wait until after Christmas to discuss it with her. By then, they could move forward without fear of mucking up their plans. Entering his apartment, he found a note under his door.

I went to bed because I was toast. Miss having your sexy body next to mine. Sweet dreams, lover. K

Smiling, he lifted it to his nose, catching a slight whiff of her jasmine body spray that always smelled so damn good. She could've just texted him, but she'd taken the time to write a note. He found it adorable. Placing it on his counter, he wistfully rubbed the paper with his finger. Admiring the cute, thoughtful gesture, he popped open one more beer and watched the rest of the game before heading to bed.

C arter's phone buzzed as he walked out of a commercial audition on Thursday afternoon.

Kayla: If I don't see you tonight, I'm going to think that you're avoiding me.

Carter laughed.

Carter: Avoiding you?? You're the one who's super busy. I was this close to breaking into your place last night and crawling into bed with you. But I think breaking and entering is a crime?

Kayla: Well, you are more than welcome to break into my house tonight. I'll be home around six and can grab dinner on the way home. Sushi, maybe? Come over around seven if that works for you.

Carter: That depends. Can I eat the sushi off your gorgeous breasts?

Kayla: It doesn't sound sanitary, exactly, but if your tongue is anywhere near my breasts, who am I to argue?

Carter could feel his smile bursting across his face.

Carter: Thanks. Now I'm hard. See you at seven. Just a note: I'm totally seducing you before sushi, so put it in the fridge. We'll devour it later...waaaaaay later...can't wait, Summers.

She sent him a kiss emoji and he realized he was smiling like a freaking idiot. Deciding he didn't give a shit, he let the excitement at seeing her course through him.

Chapter 19

♥

Kayla had barely seen Carter all week, and the day seemed to drag at work as she counted down the hours. Finally, she packed up at the office and headed home. On the way, she ordered sushi from one of the delivery apps on her phone and organized everything in the fridge once it arrived.

Noting that Carter would be over in about half an hour, she contemplated what to wear. They usually hung out in sweats, but she was feeling frisky and he'd said he was going to ravish her when he arrived. Shivering, she smiled in anticipation.

Rifling through her drawers, she pulled out the silky black nightie. She'd bought it with Laura when they'd been shopping on Fifth Avenue. Her friend had urged her to make the purchase, telling her she might find an occasion to wear it down the road. Feeling she'd never wear the skimpy thing, she eventually gave in to Laura's urging and promptly stuffed it in the back of her dresser, never to be seen again.

Lifting it high, she studied it. Black lace trailed along the edges and the material was sleek. Deciding it wouldn't hurt to try it on, she discarded her sweats and slid it over her body. Assessing her reflection, she smoothed her hands over the sides. The bulges of her love handles and abdomen were evident, but the fabric also conformed to her shape, showing off an hourglass figure. Turning, she slid her hands over her ass, noting that it certainly wasn't pert and tiny, but acknowledging that there was a sexiness about the full, round globes peeking out, especially since she wore nothing beneath.

Filled with indecision, she contemplated. Carter truly seemed to like her curves, and she felt so sexy when they were together. He'd taken a big step by committing to being monogamous and she wanted to show him that he could have great sex, even if it was only with one woman.

Deciding that taking risks had been paying off for her lately, she straightened her shoulders and headed to the bathroom. She was going to rock Carter's world and let go of her doubt. Locating the red lipstick she'd worn the night they'd had drinks with the girls, she applied it to her lips. Carter had complimented her on it and she admitted it made her lips look full and juicy.

Combing her hair, she plumped it out, flipping over and spraying some styling gel. Flipping it back, she fluffed it and smiled at her reflection. Damn, she actually looked hot.

Feeling naughty, she grabbed her favorite vibrator from the drawer—the one with the clitoral stimulator and humongous shaft—and inhaled a deep breath. Looking at her phone, she realized she had five minutes until he discovered her. Excitement coursed through her veins.

She unlocked the door and sat on the couch, sending a text to Carter.

Kayla: The door's unlocked. Come on in whenever.

Carter: Coming now. And also in about ten minutes, if I'm lucky.

Kayla threw back her head in a joyous laugh.

Kayla: I'm ready. Hope you last that long. I'm pretty horny.

Carter: Hard-on commenced. See you in one minute.

Stretching her legs out, she bent the knee that rested against the back of the couch, leaning her arm over it. Blood coursed through her body at the thought of his broad hands pulling at the silky material and she already felt wetness gathering between her thighs. Dying with anticipation, she bit her lip and waited for the doorknob to turn.

C arter reached for Kayla's front door handle, telling himself to calm down. He was aching to see her and hold her...and maybe have her look at him with those deep, gorgeous eyes as he fucked her mindless.

Opening the door, he stepped inside...and froze. Registering that he needed to shut the door, he awkwardly closed it behind him and stared at the sight before him.

Kayla, wearing the sexiest shade of sultry red on her lips, with her wavy, brown hair flowing, was dressed in some black, skimpy, silky thing that made his dick so hard, he thought it might actually detach from his body and explode.

"Hey," she said, her smile sultry. "I told you I was horny."

"Holy. Fucking. Shit." He took tentative steps toward her. She was rubbing something against the thigh of her bent knee. It looked like some sort of sex toy, but Carter had no idea. "Am I dreaming?" he asked, his voice stunned.

She bit her lip and he almost came in his pants. For the love of all that was holy, she was *magnificent*. His erection tented his sweats as he panted above her. "What's that?" he asked softly.

"Oh, this?" she asked, lifting the object and arching a brow. "This is my vibrator that you seem so enthralled with. I figured we could play with it, amongst other things, if you're so inclined."

"I'm inclined," he said, his ears ringing from the blood coursing through his body. "I'm so fucking inclined."

Laughing, she set it on the table beside the couch and lowered her feet to the floor. Gliding her palms over his hips, she stared up at him. "But, first, maybe I should take care of this for you?"

Carter's hips instinctively moved toward her, the motion unconscious but uncontrollable. Lowering her gaze to his erection, she hooked her fingers into the waistband of his pants and pushed them to his knees. Her eyes widened as she observed his near-to-bursting cock.

"Oh, my," she said, gently taking him in her hand as Carter groaned. "Yes, I think I need to take care of this right away."

Quick as lightning, he kicked off his athletic slip-ons and tore off his pants and shirt. Facing her, he slid his fingers under her chin, lifting. Placing the pad of his thumb on her lower lip, he caressed the plump skin. "You slay me, Summers. I'm dead. Look at these sexy red lips."

Her tongue darted out, licking those lips in a slow circle, washing over his thumb. "Kayla," he breathed.

Leaning forward, she took him in her hand, squeezing the base before sliding up to run the pad of her thumb over the tip. "Oh, no..." she said, her lips forming a pout. "You're leaking here." Extending her tongue, she slid the tip into the tiny hole, her brown eyes simmering.

Carter hissed a breath. "Please don't tease me, baby."

"But the build-up is the best part."

He slid his fingers into her hair, gripping as he tried to maintain control. "Please, Kayla," he begged.

Full, red lips curved as Carter realized she was going to take pity on his throbbing, desperate cock. Opening her mouth, she slid it over his engorged head.

"Fuck," he breathed, watching her slide down as far as she could, before moving back toward the head. Her cheeks hollowed as she glided, creating a suction that tightened his balls to the point of ecstasy.

Unable to stop himself, he began to jut into her, loving how she eagerly met his small thrusts with bobs of her head. Feeling his fists tighten, he reminded himself not to hurt her.

"Kayla, this is the hottest thing I've ever seen," he rasped, feeling her smile form around his straining skin at his words. "Fuck, baby. That's it. Do you like sucking my cock?"

She nodded, forcing an exclamation of joy from his heaving lungs as his hips increased their pace. "I don't want to hurt you, baby. Tell me if I'm being too rough. God, it feels so good."

She worked him like a champ, wet saliva dripping from her blood-red lips as she devoured him. Carter watched her, overcome with emotion, realizing that she was everything he'd ever wanted in a lover. How had he not pursued her for three long years? Man, he was some kind of idiot.

She mewled around his flesh, and he nudged the back of her throat with the head of his cock. "Can you try to take me deep? If it's too much, I'll pull back." She stared up at him, eyes wide and trusting, and he almost blew his load right there. "Relax your throat and tilt your head back," he commanded.

She followed his direction, something in her submission causing the animal inside him to roar. "Hold your breath when I go deep, okay, baby?" She gave a slight nod.

Tightening his hands in her hair, he pushed the head of his cock down her throat, the sensation so pleasurable that he saw stars. After only a few juts, he felt his orgasm on the horizon.

"I'm going to come, honey," he said, shaking his head in frustration. He wanted nothing more than to fuck her mouth for hours upon endless hours. "Do you want me to come in your mouth. It's okay if you don't."

He popped from her lips, his body screaming at the loss of her warm cavern, but needing to give her the ability to consent.

"Please, Carter," she said, grasping his shaft and sliding her hand over the wetness, jerking him. "Come inside my mouth. I want you to."

He cupped her chin, applying pressure to her cheeks. Her mouth opened into a perfect circle at his urging, and he slid himself back in. Gliding his hand back to her hair, he gave in to the sensation, tugging her head toward his undulating hips as he fucked her sweet mouth.

Only moments later, his balls seemed to curl up into his body and he knew he was lost. Gazing into her limitless eyes, he cried her name and began to shoot pulsing jets of release down her warm throat. Her resulting purrs drove him wild and she lapped up every drop he gave her. Feeling like a goddamn caveman, he grunted, fingers twined in her hair, claiming her with his come.

Eventually, he softened and popped himself from her mouth. Since his legs were shaking and on the verge of collapse, he lowered to the couch, his back finding the soft cushions as he reached for her. She slithered over him, snuggling into his body, and he wanted to weep with joy.

"Who are you and what have you done with my neighbor?"

Her laughter surrounded him and she nuzzled into his chest. "I've always been here. My vibrators have gotten most of my sexual attention."

"Lucky them," he muttered, placing a kiss on her forehead. "I promise I'm going to return the favor. I'm just fucking destroyed right now. I need a minute. Holy shit, Summers."

She smiled at him, so deliciously adorable, and he thought he might melt into a pile of mush. "I'm not super experienced at that. I'm glad it was good."

"Good?" he asked. "It was absolutely amazing. What's gotten into you tonight?"

She shrugged. "I just felt sexy, knowing you were going to come over and ravish me."

Feeling the corner of his lip curve, he ran his palm over the silky material. "This is so hot."

"Yeah?" she asked. "I was worried it might show some of my more...unflattering bits, but I wanted to surprise you."

He slid his fingers over her cheek. "There isn't one bit of you that's unflattering, Summers."

She grinned, rubbing the pad of her finger over his bottom lip. "When you say it, it sounds true."

"It is," he whispered, kissing her finger. "Okay, I'm ready to make you scream. Should I use the vibrator?"

"Oh, hell yes," she said, waggling her eyebrows. "We're going to have lots of fun with that."

Enveloped by her contagious energy and exquisite smile, Carter immersed himself in learning all about vibrators. And, oh, what a fantastic lesson it was.

Kayla lay on the couch, the nightie discarded somewhere on the floor, struggling to catch her breath. Carter had been enthralled by the vibrator, eyes wide as she showed him the different settings and strengths of the clitoral stimulator. He'd played with it a while, testing it against her nub as she'd held her folds apart, eyes closed in limitless pleasure. Then, he'd slipped on a condom and entered her, moving in sure strokes as he held the humming gadget to her clit. To say she'd never come so hard would be an understatement.

Now, they lay sweaty and spent upon the couch, Carter's face buried in her neck as he spooned her. They'd collapsed there when they'd both reached their peak and after he'd disposed of the condom.

Kayla's stomach growled and he chuckled against her skin. "It has to be nine o'clock at this point. We probably should eat. I say we eat naked."

Kayla laughed. "The nightie was one thing, but I'm definitely not that confident. I'm going to put on some PJs. Be right back." She placed a kiss on his arm and stood, loving how he playfully slapped her ass.

Once she'd donned the PJs, she returned to the kitchen to find him dishing out the sushi.

"I grabbed some plates and opened two beers. Dig in, Summers."

They had a fantastic dinner filled with easy conversation and laughter. Once Kayla had cleaned up the kitchen, she couldn't stifle her yawn.

"Do you mind if I stay over?" Carter asked, looking adorably handsome and a bit nervous as he waited for her response.

"I don't mind, but I need to sleep. I have to get up at five-thirty to get to the office early for this oral argument I'm working on. And, honestly, I'm pretty sore. We really went for it tonight."

Carter approached her, threading his fingers through her hair. "Woman, you just inflated my already out-of-control ego. Thank you for confirming that I'm massive and that you're incapable of taking any more." Chuckling, she rolled her eyes and he placed a kiss on her lips. "I don't care if I just hold you, Kayla. I haven't seen you all week. If you're open to me staying, I want to."

Her irises searched his, heart pounding at his words. "Okay. I have an extra toothbrush if you don't want to grab yours."

"Sounds perfect."

As she lay entwined with him, his breath even below her head on his chest, she reveled in the moment. Even if their arrangement was temporary, she was happy. Resolved to enjoy it for however long it lasted, she drifted to sleep against his warm body.

Chapter 20

♥

The next week, Kayla finally learned that she'd gotten the promotion, and everyone took her out to celebrate at a restaurant in the Flatiron district.

"You're the smartest person on Earth, Kayla," Laura said, holding
her pint glass high.

"To the queen of the briefs," Joy said.

They all clinked their glasses and Carter pulled her into his side.
"I'm so proud of you, Summers," he said, placing a kiss on her
forehead. "I'm so honored that you're my sugar mama."

Kayla laughed, throwing her head back in the sexy way that
bared the soft skin of her neck. "I *will* make a shit ton more
money now. Holy crap! I can actually afford an apartment with
an elevator!"

"Hey," Carter said, frowning at the thought of her moving out.
"Don't leave me yet, Summers. I kinda like you."

Her gorgeous smile melted his heart. "I like you too."

"Okay, barf alert," Laura joked, waving her hand between them.
"Are you guys, like, official or what?"

"I, uh..." Kayla gazed up at him. "I don't..."

"We don't need your labels, Cunningham," Carter said, calling
her by her last name. "Leave us alone."

He felt Kayla stiffen a bit in his grip, but he just wasn't ready to discuss the future yet. Although he cared about Kayla more than any woman he'd ever met, he was still apprehensive about long-term commitment and was still resolved that it was something he didn't want. Once the holidays were over, he would sit down with her privately to discuss whether they wanted to continue their relationship. Seeing that they most likely wanted different things, it didn't seem probable, and Carter felt a deep, genuine sadness at the thought of losing her.

But, she was a woman who deserved a lover and partner who could give her everything she wanted. If he couldn't do that, it was only fair to let her go. As much as he hated the thought, he had to do right by her.

Staring down at her, she gave him a smile, and he told himself to stay in the moment. For now, they had an amazing thing going and he was dedicated to ensuring they made the most of these last few days before Christmas.

That night, after they'd returned to her apartment and prepped for bed, he sensed a difference as they were making love.

"You okay, hon?" he asked, moving inside her slowly as she gazed up at him.

She nodded, but her eyes were glassy.

He froze. "What's wrong?"

Her hands dug into his back. "I don't want to lose you," she said, and his heart shattered at the gravel in her voice.

"I'm right here, baby," he said, starting to move inside her. "Can't you feel how much I want you?"

She nodded, jutting her hips toward his. Losing himself in her tight warmth, he cemented his lips to hers and brought them both to the point where they shattered.

Later, as he held her, he could've sworn he felt the wetness of a tear run across his arm. Sadness swamped him as he realized he had no way to comfort her. She was beginning to think about the future, once the holidays were over, and he just didn't know if he could offer her what she so rightly deserved. Clutching onto whatever time they had left, he held her close, reveling in the smell of her skin.

Chapter 21

♥

C hristmas Eve finally arrived and they headed to Kayla's house in Wayne. Catherine made a lovely dinner and Carter noticed that Kayla seemed relaxed and happy. She'd given him so much, and he was glad that he was able to give her an opportunity to escape from her mother's criticisms and enjoy the holiday.

It pissed him off that Catherine was so critical, inwardly noting that she'd made no less than five comments about Kayla's appearance and weight during the few hours since they'd arrived. Kayla appeared mostly unfazed, usually rolling her eyes and dismissing the off-handed statements. Carter thought she looked absolutely stunning in her dark green dress and those sexy black boots, which he knew she wore for him. The material seemed to hug every inch of her hourglass figure, showcasing her exquisite breasts and magnificent ass. He found himself aching to slide the fabric from her silky skin and cup every curve in his hands.

"So, how's your mother doing, Carter?" Bob asked from the head of the table, interrupting his thoughts.

"As good as can be expected," Carter said, smiling at Kayla as she reached over and squeezed his hand. She'd come to most of their Sunday dinners since Thanksgiving and Carter was extremely thankful that she would give up her time off to spend the day with them. It meant so much to Barbara, and seeing her happy in her final days was his number one priority.

After dinner, they gathered in the family room to exchange some presents and spend time together. Eventually, the hour grew late, and Carter and Kayla prepped for bed in her old room.

"Is it weird that I'm going to have sexual thoughts about you while we're sleeping in your parents' house?" he teased.

"Not weird at all, but there's no way I'm banging you in my childhood home, buddy."

Laughing, he pulled her close to his body after she turned off the lamp.

"I can't believe your parents are cool with putting us in the same room."

He felt her shrug. "She wasn't when Jordan first started bringing girls home for the holidays, but eventually she caved. Dad never cared either way. I think she's just so thrilled that I actually brought someone home, she'd probably supply us with condoms if we asked her."

Carter chuckled.

"Or, maybe not, since she wants me to get pregnant, like, yes-terday. She'd probably beg us to go bareback."

Kayla snickered but Carter felt his muscles stiffen.

"Sorry. Pregnancy joke. Not cool. Got it." Her voice had grown a bit solemn. "I'm not trying to trap you here, Carter. Relax."

Inhaling, he tried to ease the tension from his muscles, but it remained, sticky and pervasive.

"Do you want kids, Carter?" she asked softly.

His heart pounded in his chest as he contemplated the answer. "I don't know what you want me to say here, Kayla."

"I want you to be honest."

He nuzzled her neck with his nose. "Honestly? I've never wanted marriage or kids or any of that stuff. I like kids, and I'm not opposed to them, but I don't really like the idea of marriage, and I think that's part of the whole package. Isn't it?"

He stroked her softly, giving her time to digest his answer.

"I think that life can be what you make it. Why do you hate marriage so much?"

He told her. About his dad, and his abandonment and his complete disbelief that two people are truly meant to be together forever.

He could sense the wheels turning in her mind. "I actually agree with a lot of what you said."

"Yeah?" he asked, surprised.

She nodded. "I think that it's very improbable that two people are supposed to be together forever. But I don't think it's impossible. Most of the time, the improbable ones get carried away by lust and the excitement of marriage and I think those are the ones that are likely to fail. But I do think there are some people who truly understand how to make it work. People who allow their partners to grow and change and want to evolve with them. You've helped me change, Carter, and I don't even think you realize it."

"How?" he asked.

"You've made me realize that I'm pretty and sexy and...well, all the things I was sure I wasn't. When you look at me, when we're making love, I truly believe you think I'm beautiful."

"I do," he growled into her neck, pushing his erection into the crease of her ass.

He could sense her joy at his confirmation, and she snuggled against him. "It's an amazing gift you've given me. I'd like to give you the gift of knowing that we could build something together that won't be terrifying for you. I get that you're scared of the whole marriage, kids and suburbs thing. Hell, I am too. But it doesn't have to be the nightmare you envision. We could go at our own pace and figure it out. I don't need a map, I just need a commitment. Maybe we'll get married and stay in the city and choose to be child-free. Maybe we'll have kids. I'm not a fan of the 'burbs, so I'd actually rather raise kids in the city if I have them."

"I totally pegged you for a white picket fence girl, Summers," he said against her skin.

"I know. You have to stop prejudging me. If you tell me what you want, I'd be open to building that with you. That's what true partners do, Carter. They work to build a life that makes each other happy."

"What if I fuck it up?" he asked, strumming the skin of her forearm. "What if I build something with you and don't have the fortitude to stick with it? My dad just left and never came back. I'm so worried I'll blow it."

She surprised him by laughing, her body shaking against his. "Don't you think I'm worried I'll blow it? What if you wake up one day and decide I'm a fat troll?"

"Never," he said, smiling. "You're a goddamn sex goddess and only a fool would give that up."

Her giggle was adorable.

After a few minutes, she said, "Look, I'm pretty sure I'm in love with you, Carter." His breath caught in his throat. "I'm not saying it to scare you, but I need to know where this is going. I don't need a marriage proposal, but I need a commitment. I want you to tell people I'm your partner. In public. Everywhere. If you're not ready to do that, then you need to let me go. And you're going to have to be the one who ends it because I honestly don't have the strength to do it."

Fear warred inside him: half from the thought of losing her and half from the thought of committing to her. Unable to choose a side, he kissed her neck. "Let me think about it, okay?"

She nodded beneath him and he sensed the disappointment emanate from her lithe frame.

"You're an incredibly special woman, Kayla, and I need to make sure I can do right by you. If I can't, I need to be strong enough to let you go."

Reaching up, he wiped the tears from her cheek, hating that he was the cause of them. "Please don't cry, honey. I care about you so much. It's just so fucking complicated for me."

"I know," she said, sniffling. "You were honest with me from the start."

They held each other, and Carter prayed he had the courage to make the right choice. Whether it was choosing to commit to her or deciding she would be better off with someone whole, he just didn't know.

Chapter 22

C arter was quiet in the car on the way to his house. Knowing that he was probably reeling from their conversation last night, Kayla kept the conversation intermittent and light. When they got to his mother's house, they sat in the living room drinking eggnog before they sat down for lunch. Except for Patty, who stood and addressed the room.

"Well, everyone, I'd like to officially announce that I won't be having any eggnog today because Ryan and I are pregnant!"

Dottie jumped off the couch, running to her and giving her a warm hug. Kayla was taken with the joy on her face, hugging her and then Ryan, so thrilled to be a part of the happy moment.

Patty headed over to hug Barbara, so frail in the leather seat, and Ryan shortly thereafter.

"If it's a girl, we're going to name her Barbara, Ma," he said, cupping his mom's cheek.

"Oh, that's lovely, dear," she said, tears spilling from her eyes down her withered cheeks. "It's such an affirmation of the circle of life. I love you, son."

"Love you too, Ma," Ryan said. Kayla noticed that his eyes were swimming with tears. After they devoured their lunch, Patty grabbed Kayla's wrist.

"I need to chat with this one," she said, tugging Kayla upstairs. Once there, they sat on Barbara's bed as Patty studied her.

"So, I sense something different with you and Carter today. Are you guys okay?"

Kayla nodded. "We had a pretty intense talk last night. As I'm sure you've figured out, our fake relationship kind of took a sexual turn."

"Ohhh..." Patty said, waggling her eyebrows.

"Yeah," Kayla said, chuckling. "But I told him last night I need more. That I need a commitment. I don't need a proposal or anything like that—I mean, this is still fairly new—but I need to know he sees some sort of future with me. Otherwise, I don't think I can carry on. Even though the sex is unbelievable." She shrugged, giving Patty a shy grin.

"I get it, girl," Patty said. "Carter's one of those guys who thinks he loves being a player but inside, he's mush."

"He is," she said, nodding. "He says the sweetest things to me when we're together. He'd make such a great boyfriend. But I don't want to force him. I'd rather let him go than have him resent me."

"Man, you're really evolved, Kayla," she said, laughing. "Most women would try to change a man in a second. You really love him for who he is."

"I really do," she said. "Wow. I love him. It's so strange. I haven't been in love...well, maybe ever. Holy shit."

"It's amazing when you find the right person. Look," Patty said, sliding her hand over Kayla's. "I'm not sure if Carter's going to be able to give you what you want. He's really fucked up from his dad's abandonment. But I think you're doing the right thing. As we can see from Barbara," her expression grew sad, "there's no time to waste. I'm proud of you for having the courage to make him choose."

Kayla took a sip of her eggnog, thankful for Patty's perspective.

And hoping with all her might that Carter would choose her.

"W hat are you doing, Carter?" Ryan asked.

"Excuse me?" Carter asked, almost finished raking the leaves that had previously been scattered over his mom's back-yard.

"With Kayla. She's fucking amazing, bro. I'm not sure if you've looked lately, but you're dating a gorgeous attorney who you men-tioned to me a couple of times is a tiger in bed. So, I'll ask you again—what the hell are you doing? I sense the tension between you guys. Are you really going to let her walk away after this stupid holiday deal you made is over?"

Sighing, Carter gripped the handle of the rake and rested his hand on his hip. "I don't want to get married, Ryan. Look how that worked out for Mom and Dad."

"Yes, marriages fail sometimes. That's life, man. But what's the point if you don't try?"

Carter sighed. "It always came so easy to you, Ry. You always wanted the whole wife and kids thing. You know I never did."

Ryan sat on the wooden bench by the chain-link fence, gesturing for Carter to sit beside him. Once he did, he stared off in the distance, appearing to consider his words.

"I cheated on Patty," he finally said.

"What?" Carter asked, shock reverberating through him. "When?"

Ryan sighed. "When we first got engaged. I was just so over-whelmed with all the changes in my life. I'd just gotten my PA license and work was busy. She'd given me an ultimatum that she was moving on if I didn't propose, so I did." He ran his hands over his face. "I went out with a buddy one night and we met these two chicks. I hooked up with one in her car. Didn't have sex, but it got pretty heavy before I gathered my wits and headed home.

"Patty knew right away. She kicked me out on my ass and I realized what a stupid fucking mistake I'd made." Lifting his gaze to Carter's, he said, "You see, man, it hasn't always come easy to me. I let you believe that because I was the oldest and I wanted to be strong for you, but Dad leaving fucked me up too. I was so sure that I had absolutely no foundation to be a husband so I subconsciously sabotaged the best thing that ever happened to me."

"Holy shit, Ry," Carter said. "I had no idea."

"Yeah," he said, swiping some dirt from his jeans. "Once I realized my mistake, I set about making it right. I've never worked so hard to gain someone's forgiveness. In the end, she loved me enough to take me back. And you know what? She really let it go. I'm so fucking lucky."

Turning, he placed his hand on Carter's shoulder. "I don't want you to make the same mistake I did, sabotaging something because you think you don't have the programming to make it work. If you find the right person, you can always make it work, Carter."

He breathed a laugh. "It's funny. Kayla said the same thing to me last night."

"I know you think marriage is a losing bet but, the thing is, marriage to the right person is actually fucking awesome. Take it from me. Patty and I are so damn happy. It's more than I ever imagined."

"What about the whole 'one vagina for life' thing?" Carter asked, only half-joking. "Doesn't it freak you out that she's the last woman you're ever going to sleep with?"

"Hell no!" Ryan said. "The sex with her is a hundred times better than any woman I've ever been with. Why would I give that up for mediocre sex with someone I don't know? I love that I know her hot buttons and how to make her scream. And afterward, she looks at me like I'm a goddamned superhero. It's fucking amazing."

Carter thought of all the times he'd held Kayla, craving her soft body against his. "Kayla's the first woman I've ever slept with. You know, without having sex. Sometimes we just hold each other and fall asleep. It's so strange to me."

"But does it feel good?"

Carter couldn't control his smile. "It feels fucking unbelievable. I can't get enough of her skin and her smell...I don't know how I'm going to live without it."

"Then don't let her go."

"But how can I promise her marriage and kids and all that stuff when I don't want it myself?"

"Is she asking you to promise her that?"

His eyebrows drew together. "No. She said that, right now, she just wants a commitment. That we'll figure out the rest down the road."

"Dude, you're insane. I swear to god, if you fuck this up, I'm disowning you as my brother. Make the fucking commitment to her then! She's literally offering you a perfect compromise. And, yes, you'll figure it out. These things always find a way of evolving organically."

Carter inhaled a deep breath, digesting his brother's words. "I'll think about it, Ry. It's all I can do for now. Less than two months ago, I was a single guy getting his rocks off with super-hot chicks on a consistent basis. Now, I have this incredible woman who wants me to settle down. It's a massive change."

"It is," he said with a nod. "But you're thirty-five years old, Carter. Do you want to be banging random chicks at forty? Fifty? Or do you want to be with someone who absolutely adores you and puts you first? It's not even a contest in my mind."

"Thanks, bro," Carter said, patting him on the back. "You've given me a lot to think about. And thank goodness Patty took you back. She's definitely your better half."

"You speak the truth," Ryan said with a laugh.

Determined to finish piling the leaves before the sun set, Carter sent his brother inside so he could finish the task and contemplate his words.

C arter hugged his mom as she sat in the chair, so sad to leave her, but needing to get home. The studio was cheaper the day after Christmas and he'd booked it to record a new audiobook he'd just signed on to narrate.

"I really enjoyed this Christmas, Ma," he said. "Love you so much."

"I love you, dear boy," she said.

Kayla leaned down and gave her a hug. "You're a really special woman, Ms. Manheim," she said softly. "Thanks for raising such an awesome son."

"Thank you for loving him," she whispered, cupping Kayla's cheek.

Kayla nodded and Carter observed her struggle with tears.

The air during the ride home was heavy. Kayla reached over and enfolded his hand in hers. He threaded their fingers together, taking comfort from her.

When they arrived home, he followed her into her apartment, drained and weary.

"Here," she said, taking his coat. "You look exhausted. Want to chill on the couch?"

"Yeah," he said. "Actually, I'm going to go next door and throw on sweats." Grabbing his coat, he smiled. "I'll be back in a few."

"Okay," she said, concern evident in her eyes.

As he changed, he contemplated his brother's words. Sitting on his bed, he ran his fingers through his hair, frustrated at his indecision. He wanted so badly to make a commitment to Kayla, but something was holding him back. Realizing that she deserved better, he lifted his phone and dialed her number.

"Hey," she said. He could hear her voice through the wall and realized she was in her bedroom.

"Hey," he said, lifting his hand to the wall, aching to connect with her. "I'm really tired. I think I'm just gonna turn in over here."

"Okay," she said.

Sighing, he shook his head, searching for words. "There's just so much going on, Kayla. With my mom and the audition in January."

"I know," she said, and he noticed a latent resolve in her voice. "Remember when I said I wasn't strong enough to end it? That you had to be the one who did it for me?"

"Yes," he whispered, feeling a sense of dread set in.

"Well, I actually am strong enough. You made me stronger, Carter, and I'll always love you for that, but I just can't do this."

"Kayla," he whispered.

"I truly wish you the best, Carter. These few weeks have been amazing. You're the best fake boyfriend I ever could've asked for."

"It wasn't fake to me, Kayla. You have to know that."

"I do," she said. His heart shuddered at the tears in her voice. "It wasn't fake for me either. Don't make it weird, okay?"

He gave a warbled laugh. "Okay, Summers."

"See ya in the hallway. Remember, shirtless garbage disposal is mandatory."

"Got it," he said, barely able to say the words since his throat was clogged with emotion.

"Night."

"Night."

The phone went dead and he looked at the wall, running his fingers over it, wishing it was her skin. Something wet fell on his chest and he realized it was a tear. Holy shit. Carter couldn't remember crying in his entire adult life. Exhausted, he collapsed on the bed, unable to process anything else but sleep.

Chapter 23

♥

Kayla did her best to buck up and move on. She'd fallen in love with Carter, but she'd pretty much known that was going to happen the second their relationship turned sexual. Chalking it up to a life lesson learned, and sex with the hottest guy she'd probably ever encounter, she carried on.

Laura and Joy seemed amazed at her composure, offering to stuff her full of rocky road and watch Hugh Grant movies until their tear ducts bled, but she refused. Even though she'd expected to feel devastated, she'd gained a strength from Carter that she was truly thankful for. She found herself much less critical of her appearance and had a newfound confidence that made her feel like she could take on the world.

After spending New Year's Eve with her amazing best friends, she set forth to conquer new heights in January. Since her promotion, she'd gained a new vigor at work, and she reveled in each case assigned to her.

She rarely saw Carter in the building and wondered if he was spending more time at home. In mid-January, she received a text from Patty.

Patty: I literally had to steal your number from Carter's phone, but I got it. This is Patty, by the way. Barbara passed away last night and I thought you might want to come to the funeral. It's

**this Saturday at St. Patrick's in Pompton Lakes. There will be a
service at her home afterward.**

Kayla didn't even try to stop the tears from streaming down her
face. She immediately thought of Carter, her heart breaking at the
pain he must be experiencing.

**Kayla: Thank you so much, Patty. I'll be there. Please give
everyone my love.**

When Saturday arrived, she called the rideshare and showed up
to the church, honored to be able to pay respects to the woman
whom she'd only known a short time, but who'd raised the man
she would always love deep in a corner of her heart.

Entering the church, she saw Carter standing beside Ryan and
Patty.

"Hey," she said, smiling up at him. "I'm so sorry."

The surprise of her appearance was evident on his face. "Hey,"
he said, his smile so tender, causing her heart to melt. "I didn't
realize you were coming."

"Of course, I wanted to come. I told you I'd always be here for
you, Carter."

He surrounded her with his arms, holding her in a tight embrace.
"Thank you, Kayla. It's so amazing that you're here. I've missed
you so much."

Pulling back, she wiped a tear from her cheek. "I've missed you
too."

"Thank you for coming," Ryan said. She hugged him and then
wrapped her arms around Patty.

"Thanks for texting me."

"Sure thing," she said, squeezing.

Giving one last smile of support to Carter, Kayla headed down
the aisle and sat in the pew.

Once the service was over, she called a rideshare home. Writing a note of support to Carter, she slipped it under his door, knowing he would get it in a few days when he came home.

T he weeks forged along and Kayla continued to crush it at work. One night in early February, she was working on a brief in her PJs, feet curled under her on the couch, when she heard a knock at the door. Setting her laptop aside, she plodded to the door, pulling it open to find Carter on the other side. He was dressed in a sweater, jeans and loafers and had a goofy grin on his face. Holding up a stack of small papers, he shook them.

"You're slacking, Summers," he said.

Elation coursed through her as she reveled in his presence.

"Slacking?" she asked.

"You were slipping notes under my door with a fair amount of regularity, but I haven't gotten one in days. What gives?"

Throwing back her head, she laughed. "I've been really busy. Work has been insane."

"I live for these notes, Summers. You hold my happiness in your hands."

"I do?" she asked softly.

His smile was so reverent. "You always have." His eyes darted over her. "Can I come in?"

"Oh, sure," she said, stepping back. "I opened some wine. Want some?"

"Sure," he said, sliding into one of the stools at the counter. She grabbed her wine glass from the table beside the couch and refilled it along with a glass for him. Standing on the other side of the island, she lifted her glass. "To your happiness."

Laughing, he clinked his glass with hers. "To *our* happiness." His gaze bore into her as he sipped, causing butterflies to flutter in her stomach.

"You look nice," she said, thinking he looked delicious in the semi-casual wear. "Hot date?"

"Not really. I was celebrating with my agent. I got the part, Kayla."

"The theater role?" she asked. He nodded. "Oh, my god! That's fantastic, Carter! I'm so happy for you."

"Thanks," he said, his grin almost shy. "I didn't think I had a shot in hell, but my agent said they absolutely adored my audition."

"Wow. That's incredible. You're going to be a famous actor. I can say I knew you when."

Chuckling, he shrugged. "I'll never be as amazing as you. How's the promotion treating you?"

"Good. I'm making gobs of money and really enjoy the different types of cases I'm being given. My lease is up in March and I'm going to finally find an apartment with a damn elevator."

His face fell and she lifted her shoulders, feeling as if she'd hurt him somehow. "I was going to tell you. Plus, it's probably easier if I don't catch you in the hallway with any of your Amazonian supermodels. Jealous ex-fake-girlfriend and all."

He looked so sad that she reached across and grabbed his wrist. "One of us was bound to move out eventually, Carter. We can still meet up. You can always text me."

"So, you're really done with me?" he asked softly.

Kayla swallowed. "I..." she struggled for words. "I thought you were really done with me."

He sighed, slow and morose, resting his forehead on his fingers. "I was never done with you, Kayla. I was just really fucked up. It was just so much, with my mom and how fast things were moving. I couldn't handle it and shut down."

"I completely understand, Carter. I don't blame you. We were just the product of shitty timing. Who knows? I might still need a fake boyfriend next year. My prospects aren't exactly vast."

He blinked, appearing to contemplate his next words. "I changed up my monologue."

"For the audition?" she asked, confused.

"Yes. I ended up writing my own."

"Oh, wow. I didn't know you wrote too."

"I didn't. Until you." Standing, he pulled a folded piece of paper out of his pocket. "It's written here, but I have it memorized. Want to hear it?"

Kayla's heart thrummed in her chest, and she wondered why she was so nervous. "Sure," she said, her throat scratchy.

"Come sit over here," he said, extending his hand. She took it and he led her to the couch. "It's better if you're comfortable."

"Okay," she said, folding her leg underneath as she cozied into the couch. "Go for it."

He straightened his spine and inhaled a deep breath. Focusing on the window behind her, he began to speak, his tone practiced and reverent.

"At night, I would call to her, through the wall that separated our rooms. Stroking it with my hand, I would tell her how sorry I was and how much I missed her smile. Finally, I realized that she would never hear my words. Never feel my silent caress as it longed to flow against her skin."

His gaze fell to hers and Kayla watched him through tear-filled eyes, her chin trembling.

"I understood that she was lost to me and that I'd let go of the one thing that made me whole. While I had been so scared of being broken, I was too blinded by fear to realize she was the one who completed the puzzle. The one who filled the gaps.

"And now, I've lost her, as the ancient gods lost Atlantis to the sea, and all I can do is weep soundless tears and wish her well, hoping she finds someone who will fill the brokenness I've now created in her soul."

Kayla pulled her knees to her chest, burying her face in them as she sobbed. His strong arms surrounded her, pulling her into his firm body.

"Don't cry, baby," his deep voice said in her ear. "Please. It breaks my heart when you cry."

"That was so beautiful," she said, lifting her face to his. "How could you write something so beautiful?"

"Love makes you do some pretty intense things, Summers," he said, cupping her jaw with his hands and wiping the wetness with the pads of his thumbs.

"Love?" she whispered.

"Yeah," he said, the corners of his lips curling. "I'm kind of obsessed with you, Kayla. I figured someone as smart as you would've realized that by now."

"But you don't want a commitment. You love your single life. I don't want to change you, Carter. You would resent me and that would be worse than forging on without you."

He shook his head, gazing at her so reverently. "Do you know how many men wish they could fall in love with a woman who doesn't want to change them? I can name about five of my friends off the top of my head."

Kayla laughed. "It's true. I love who you are. I just can't be in a relationship that has no chance of a future. I need a commitment that we're building something together."

"Then I'll give it to you," he said, the words so simple they took her breath away. "I'm not ready to promise marriage or kids and, honestly, I don't know if I'll ever be. But I can promise to spend every day putting you first and doing my best to make you happy.

And you're wrong about one thing. I realized that I don't love being single anymore. The thought of holding anyone else the way I'm holding you now has zero appeal to me. You've ruined me, Summers. I should be livid." He winked.

"Oh, no," she said, giggling. "Are you mad that I might be the last person you ever sleep with?"

"I was, for a while, until I realized that only a fool wouldn't be one hundred percent on board with that. As long as we use the vibrator on occasion." He waggled his eyebrows. "Oh, and I need the red lipstick to be applied during one out of every three blow jobs."

Laughter burst from her throat. "Done. But I need shirtless Sundays in the house. And every other day too, if I'm being honest."

His body shook with laughter. Placing his forehead against hers, he said, "I'm sorry it's not more, but it's what I can give right now."

"It's all I need, Carter. We'll get there. As long as we love each other, that's all that matters."

"Kayla," he whispered, brushing her lips with his. "I love you so much. I'm so sorry I had to hurt you to get here. I just needed to process it in my own way."

"I love you too and will probably forgive you," she said, teasing him. "It will definitely help if you make love to me. Any surface of your choice is appropriate."

His lips captured hers, moving in sure strokes as he plundered her with his tongue. Gently biting her lip, he said, "I never got to take you from behind. I want to lay you over the couch and cup that gorgeous ass and fuck you from behind."

Kayla literally gushed in her pants. "Well, someone has a fantasy."

"About your delectable ass?" he asked, nuzzling her nose with his. "I have about a million. Buckle up, baby. If you're the only woman I'm with, we're going to take full advantage."

Throwing back her head, she laughed. "Oh, Carter, you say the sweetest things."

"Don't push me, Summers. I might even write a rom-com next."

Pressing her lips to his, she sighed. "A girl can only dream."

There, entwined on the couch, they lost themselves in their tender yet passionate caresses, cementing the first official day of their non-fake-relationship.

Before You Go!

W ell, dear readers, I hope you loved Kayla and Carter as much as I did! Want to see them again *and* see Joy fall in love? You can read Joy's book, **Her Valentine Surprise**, right now!

P lease consider leaving a review on Amazon, BookBub and/or Goodreads. Your reviews help spread the word for indie authors so we can keep writing smokin' hot books for you to devour. Thanks so much for reading!

About the Author

♥

Ayla Asher is the contemporary pen name for a USA Today bestselling author who writes steamy fantasy romance under a different pseudonym. However, she loves a spicy, fast-paced contemporary romance too! Therefore, she's decided to share some of her contemporary stories, hoping to spread a little joy one HEA at a time. She would love to connect with you on social media, where she enjoys making dorky TikToks, FB/IG posts and steamy book trailers!

ALSO BY AYLA ASHER

Made in the USA
Middletown, DE
14 December 2023

44585457R00099